THE PROBLEM WITH PROPHECIES

THE
CELIA CLEARY
SERIES

THE PROBLEM WITH PROPHECIES

SCOTT REINTGEN

ALADDIN

New York London Toronto Sydney New Delhi

ALADDIN

An imprint of Simon & Schuster Children's Publishing Division
1230 Avenue of the Americas, New York, New York 10020
First Aladdin hardcover edition May 2022
Text copyright © 2022 by Scott Reintgen
Jacket illustration copyright © 2022 by Julie McLaughlin
All rights reserved, including the right of reproduction in whole or in part in any form.
ALADDIN and related logo are registered trademarks of Simon & Schuster, Inc.
For information about special discounts for bulk purchases, please contact
Simon & Schuster Special Sales at 1-866-506-1949 or business@simonandschuster.com.
The Simon & Schuster Speakers Bureau can bring authors to your live event. For more
information or to book an event contact the Simon & Schuster Speakers Bureau
at 1-866-248-3049 or visit our website at www.simonspeakers.com.
Book designed by Laura Lyn DiSiena
The text of this book was set in Urge Text.
Manufactured in the United States of America 0422 FFG
2 4 6 8 10 9 7 5 3 1
Library of Congress Cataloging-in-Publication Data
Names: Reintgen, Scott, author.
Title: The problem with prophecies / Scott Reintgen.
Description: First Aladdin hardcover edition. | New York : Aladdin, 2022. |
Series: The Celia Cleary series ; 1 | Audience: Ages 10 to 14. | Summary: "Twelve-year-old
Celia Cleary's first vision launches a quest to change her neighbor Jeffrey Johnson's
fate"—Provided by publisher.
Identifiers: LCCN 2021042493 (print) | LCCN 2021042494 (ebook) |
ISBN 9781665903578 (hc) | ISBN 9781665903592 (ebook)
Subjects: CYAC: Fate and fatalism—Fiction. | Prophecies—Fiction. | Death—Fiction. |
Grandmothers—Fiction. | Magic—Fiction. | LCGFT: Novels.
Classification: LCC PZ7.1.R4554 Pr 2022 (print) | LCC PZ7.1.R4554 (ebook) | DDC [Fic]—dc23
LC record available at https://lccn.loc.gov/2021042493
LC ebook record available at https://lccn.loc.gov/2021042494

To Scottie Reintgen,

I am already rearranging my heart.

Making additions. Great sprawling rooms that

I know will be filled with your light.

Welcome to the world, little one.

CONTENTS

CHAPTER ONE

The 4,444th Day

Most people expect seers to live somewhere *weird*. A creepy house on the corner with roses that never bloom. Some lonely farm with a hunched roof. Anything mysterious.

Which is why people are always surprised by Grammy's very suburban townhome. It's just so plain. I like watching her customers park on the side of the road. They always check their phones to make sure they've got the right address. Could that *really* be it? It's not painted midnight black. No cobwebs on the front porch. What kind of seer lives in a house like that? And how could they be any good?

Eventually the customers climb out of their cars. They'll look up and down the sidewalk before crossing our well-manicured lawn, starting up our well-swept steps, and knocking with a handle that's disappointingly *not* in the shape of a gargoyle.

Grammy takes great pleasure in making her first appearance. She's in her seventies now, but walks every single day and has an eye for what's fashionable. Most of her customers take a look at her and their doubts double in size. No crystal ball? No pointed hat? No cats slinking in the background?

"Expectations are their own kind of magic," Grammy always tells me.

So the customer enters. Grammy allows the disappointment to grow. She sits them on a normal-looking couch, gives them a normal cup of coffee, and doesn't ask them to pay in vials of blood or anything weird. A credit card will work just fine, thank you. And at the exact moment that the customer's doubt has reached a peak, Grammy invites them into the world of magic.

I like watching them leave as much as I like watching them arrive. Some walk out with a haunted expression. Others leave with a face-splitting grin. It's a miracle any of them can drive away without crashing straight into the bushes, because every single one of them leaves with a little slice of the future in their pocket.

For better or for worse.

But today there are no customers scheduled. I sit by my window upstairs and watch as the other neighborhood kids head for the bus stop. Jordan Lyles comes up one side of the street. He's wearing his chrome headphones and carefully avoiding puddles and fallen leaves so his new sneakers remain in pristine condition. The Kapowski sisters have to chase their little rat terrier—Chutney—down the steps of their house on the corner. It takes them a minute to usher him back inside before they head out the door themselves. Next to arrive is quiet Jeffrey Johnson. He's carrying his soccer bag up the hill like it's full of bricks.

The last person to join the crowded corner is Avery. A

knot forms in my stomach. It's been almost eight months since we last talked. Way back at the very start of the school year. We were standing in the park near the bus stop. I can still remember how bright red her cheeks had gotten, how loud our voices echoed. All I was trying to do was help, and she blamed me for everything.

A part of me is still mad at her. A bigger part misses her. On today of all days, it would be nice to have my best friend at my side. Instead, I watch as the bus arrives to pick them up. Everyone is out there except for me. The doors rattle closed and the engine rumbles and they vanish around a corner.

I'm not going to school today because it's the 4,444th day of my life.

Mom called the front office and told them I was sick. Grammy has been humming excitedly to herself all week. It's not like I woke up with horns or anything like that. But this day has always been very important in the Cleary family, stretching back through the generations. It is the day that I will see my first prophecy. It is the day that every alternating generation of Clearys sees their very first vision.

Taking a deep breath, I head downstairs. Mom's voice echoes from the front office area. She's working from home for my big day. I reach the bottom step and glance back through the hallway. I'm surprised to see she's fully dressed, even wearing her nice shoes. It's just like Mom to want to look the part, even if she's not going into the office.

Mom isn't magical, at least not in the way that I will be. Our prophetic gifts always skip a generation. Which means no magic, no prophecies, nothing at all. I'm pretty sure reality suits her, though. She's one of the best attorneys in town. Last year one of her cases was even made into a documentary. Everyone knows her name in our area. I pause in the hallway to listen for a second.

"Look," she's saying. "Allen hasn't even done his due diligence . . . No, I don't think . . ."

I can't help grinning as I imagine whoever is on the other end of the line. Even without magic, Mom is a force of nature. Always getting the job done. I continue into the kitchen.

Grammy stands with her back to me in front of the stovetop. She's got a huge mixing bowl planted on one hip, and her hair is up in a messy bun. She thrusts the mixing spoon into the air without looking back, accidentally splashing a little egg yolk.

"I predict someone is here for omelets!"

I take a seat at the kitchen table. "And I predict . . . that something is burning."

Grammy curses as she slams the bowl down and darts over to the toaster. She juggles the dead toast onto the nearest plate and examines it.

"We have the technology. We can rebuild him!"

I laugh as she starts using a knife to scrape away the burnt sections. Sliding out of my chair, I cross over to the kitchen counter. Before she's in too deep, I unravel the bread tie and hand her two more slices.

"I predict these will do better."

With a nod of concession, Grammy clears the plate and starts fresh. "So. Are you excited about your *big* day, Celia? Skipping school, burnt toast! It's already off to a promising start."

I'm not sure how to feel. My hands have been shaking

a little all morning. Grammy is always saying that a first prophecy is kind of like a first birthday. Almost like starting a whole new life. I've been waiting for this day since I was three years old. I've always wanted to be just like Grammy.

Until the fight with Avery.

It just so happens that the argument that ended our friendship was about my family's magic. I can still hear words like *fake* and *freak*. I've tried to tell myself that she was just mad when she said what she said—that she didn't mean it—but she hasn't spoken to me since.

The Cleary family has possessed the gift of prophecy for centuries. My ancestors have been navigators and military strategists and talk show hosts. Some used their ability to see the future to do good—like Grammy—and quietly blended into the real world. Others ended up being notorious outlaws or hermits.

When I was little, I used to ask Grammy about cauldrons and broomsticks. Like a lot of people, I thought being a seer would look like what I saw in cartoons. She patiently explained that families like ours inspired the modern idea of a witch, but that once the concept was in Hollywood's hands, there was no chance of accuracy. Actual seers have the future and a few minor spells at their disposal. We were not, she insisted, running around with wands casting bolts of lightning at each other. At the time, I was pretty disappointed. Lightning bolts sounded fun.

Grammy never denied that there could be other magical users out there in the world, but she suspected the most powerful branches had faded centuries ago.

"Even seers," she told me, "are a dying breed. There are very few families like us. Most didn't treat this gift as something worth preserving at all costs. Instead, they stamped out their strangeness. It's easier to fit in with everyone else than it is to shine in your own way."

After the fight with Avery, I could understand someone wanting to hide their abilities to fit in. But I've waited for this day my entire life. I'm nervous, honestly, because a part of me knows this could be my chance to prove Avery wrong and to use my powers for good. Maybe it's my chance to win her back too.

"I'm excited," I finally answer. "Tell me about your first prophecy again."

It's one of my favorite stories. Grammy empties her bowl into the skillet, spins it back onto the counter, and turns to me. She's always thrilled to tell this story, because it's her favorite too.

"Well, I was living in Asheville. Our family was a little bigger back then. Take your five wild cousins and multiply by five. Our house was always full of people. I kind of felt like I was floating. Talking with everyone, but not really hearing what they said. And then there was this moment where I felt *cold*. That crisp feeling you get when you go up into the mountains. And without warning, the entire room vanished.

"All I could see was this gorgeous red rose. A single thorn. Lovely petals. It was so beautiful. Some of my cousins had already had their first visions. And of course I'd spent months listening to them retell their stories. Some of them could walk around their vision and examine every angle. Others could change the details! Not me. All I could see was that perfect image of a red, red rose. It was another ten years before I saw it again."

"Grandpa," I say with a smile. "The day you met Grandpa."

"He was plenty handsome," she says. "But when he held out that rose, I almost fainted. It was *exactly* the way I remembered it. Now, keep in mind that not *everyone* sees through a romantic lens. There are plenty of branches of magic. My cousin Tessa is a genius with weather. My grandma was a Doomspeak. So don't go assuming you're supposed to go off and get hitched to some stranger."

I roll my eyes. "No worries there, Grammy."

She's about to offer another piece of advice, but Mom's arrival in the kitchen cuts her off. Business heels click along the hardwoods. Mom pours a cup of coffee, carefully mixing in a healthy dose of creamer. I frown when I realize it's a travel mug. Grammy notices too. Mom turns around and she's already wearing an apologetic smile.

"I'm so sorry, Celia. Someone has royally screwed up something at work. I'm afraid if I don't go in, we're going to be dealing with the fallout for *weeks*."

I nod back, a little too quickly. "Yeah. No problem."

She doubles down by throwing out a bottom lip. "I know it's your big day, honey. Really. I'm so sorry. But I'll try to leave work early. We'll watch a good movie tonight to celebrate. Sip some hot chocolate. You can tell me all about your vision, okay?"

I nod again. "That's perfect. Seriously."

She kisses my forehead and sweeps back out of the room. I can feel Grammy watching me as we both listen to the noises of leaving. The light jingle of house keys. Doors groaning open and closed. The car firing up in the garage. I don't realize, at first, that I'm tearing off little strips from a napkin on the table. I set the pieces aside and look up. Grammy is still watching.

"I've never told you this," she says. "But my mother missed my first vision. She didn't need a disaster at work to slip away either. They found her picking scuppernongs out in one of our back fields. Try not to blame your mother too much. It's a hard day for someone who will never taste magic."

It makes all the sense in the world, but I have to look back down at the napkin and tear off more strips to keep myself from crying. Grammy seems on the verge of saying more when a loud beep sounds. Two slices of absurdly burnt toast appear. The sight of them breaks the gloomy spell. Grammy and I exchange a look before bursting into belly laughter.

"Come one, come all," she thunders between laughs. "Witness the seer who can burn toast!"

CHAPTER TWO

The First Vision

After conquering toast and omelets, Grammy insists on a good long walk. We march down our favorite section of the greenway. The shaded path winds between our neighborhood and another one. Right behind our house, there's a wooden bridge that stretches over a small creek. I've always loved the way that everything gets quieter when we cross to the other side. All the noise of cars and roads, briefly muted by the surrounding trees. It's like the greenway is inviting us into some time long ago.

But the usual calm doesn't come today. I can't calm

the nervous energy that's gaining momentum inside me. Grammy notices. She guides us back down the trail and into the house. She sits me down in the living room, lights a single candle, and plays one of her old records.

It's the right kind of quiet.

We sit there for almost an hour.

I almost bolt to my feet when the phone rings. Grammy takes the call in the other room. From the sound of the conversation, I can tell it's a client desperate for a visit. Grammy kindly delays the appointment to another day before hanging up. I'm thankful when she plunks back down beside me on the couch.

"You could take a few customers," I say, trying to be polite. "We might be waiting all day."

Grammy scowls. "You must be outside of your little mind. It's an honor to watch more magic come into this world. It has precious little of it, Celia. I would not miss this for the world."

I smile before letting my head rest against the side of her leg. Grammy usually offers vague advice to her clients. She always says caution is necessary when handing people the future. But I'm grateful she's never vague with me. There's never a hidden agenda. Just honesty and love.

We spend the next few hours playing board games. I work on a few homework assignments while she spends time knitting. Grammy calls it SBT time—separate but together. She makes more coffee, but doesn't let me have any. Apparently, one of her cousins drank espresso before her first vision and almost time-traveled. We're halfway through our third game of cards when the smell of a campfire comes from nowhere.

I glance at Grammy's candle and blink. It's labeled as lavender. But that smell . . .

"Celia?"

The air tastes like toasted marshmallows. Thick with smoke. And I can feel myself *falling*.

Grammy vanishes. The living room *pops* out of existence. The world colors back in around me. I stand there, carefully drinking in every detail. I'm on a familiar country road. A shiver runs down my spine when I realize I'm standing right in the *middle* of the road, both feet set neatly on one of those painted yellow lines. Cones run down the left side of my vision. Beyond them, I spy train tracks. The familiarity finally clicks. I know this place.

It's Green Chapel Road. Right outside our neighborhood.

There's movement. It's almost like someone unpausing a show on Netflix. The road suddenly fills with life. I see a car moving from the direction of downtown. Another car's driving the opposite way. And in the distance is a boy. My mind stumbles over the sight, because he's even more famil-iar than the road. I know those hunched shoulders. I know those dangling soccer cleats.

My quiet seventh-grade neighbor: Jeffrey Johnson.

For a brief and impossible moment, I wonder if I'm sup-posed to marry Jeffrey? But the thought leaves as quickly as it came. That's not what I'm seeing. This isn't like Grammy's rose at all. With no more effort than a thought, my ghostly form glides down the road. I move faster than the speeding cars. Momentum pulls me within twenty feet of Jeffrey.

He's got his backpack dangling from his left hand. He's wisely walking in the opposite direction of traffic, carefully striding well clear of the shoulder.

And then it happens.

The car heading downtown clips one of the traffic cones. The driver panics, swerving just enough to spook the driver coming the other way. There's a squeal of tires. Jeffrey looks up at the exact moment that the second car switches directions. And the driver can't correct in time.

The air tastes like ashes. Like something burning. The scene vanishes. Grammy has me in her arms, whispering quietly, moving me so that I'm sitting back on the couch.

"You're back now, Celia. You're back."

My eyes widen. Grammy's waiting with an expectant smile, but my words wipe the expression off her face. "Jeffrey Johnson," I gasp. "He's going to die."

CHAPTER THREE

As Fate Would Have It

Grammy just *barely* stops me from barreling out the door.

"Celia! Hold on! Just wait!"

I spin back around and realize I'm not even sure what my plan is. My first thought was to get to school, intercept Jeffrey before the accident happens. Grammy's beat-up Accord is in the garage. She doesn't drive much these days, but I know she's my best bet. The image of Jeffrey Johnson is pulsing in my head like a painting that's come to life.

"He's going to die, Grammy. I need you to drive me to school."

I snatch her keys from the hook on the wall. My desperation doesn't seem to be getting through to Grammy. She's standing there with her arms crossed.

"Celia." Grammy's voice is sharp. "Sit."

There's something almost magnetic about the command. My feet carry me back into the living room, and I plunk down on the couch. I stare defiantly back at Grammy.

"Did you just use magic on me?"

"It's an old spell," she replies. "Known only by mothers, grandmothers, and teachers. It's called having a firm voice. I need you to take a breath. Listen to me, honey. You've been on this earth for 4,444 days. I'd like to think you spent most of those days *trusting* my opinion. Correct?"

I sigh impatiently. "Yes."

"Okay. What did you see? Just walk me through the details."

I explain the vision to her and note that Jeffrey Johnson is one of my classmates. She nods along like I'm telling her what the weather's going to be today. When I finally finish, it takes all the effort I have not to shove the keys into her hands and demand we get moving. Jeffrey Johnson is going to die, and I *have* to save him. Time is not on my side.

"Oh dear," Grammy says.

My eyes fix on her. *Oh dear*? Is that really all she has to say? Grammy has always been the kindest person I know. She's the person who brightens the world—my world. But there's not much compassion in those two words, or in her current expression.

"What?" I ask impatiently. "What is it?"

"It's a death prophecy."

"I figured that out already."

"Fate has decided," Grammy explains. "Most futures come with a probability. There are ways to sway what can and will happen. Death is another matter. We cannot beat death. I am quite certain you'll have heard me say the words before. *As fate would have it*." She lets out the deepest sigh I've ever heard. "Those aren't just words to us. When it comes to death visions, fate *will* have its way. It has shown you what will happen. I know this is a bitter pill to swallow, Celia."

I frown. "What's the point of the vision if I'm not allowed to change it?"

"You're allowed to do whatever you want. It just won't work the way you think it will."

"Can you take me to school or not, Grammy?"

I dangle the keys out, hoping she'll take them. She offers a face full of pity. I watch in disbelief as she shakes her head. Would she really just let this happen? I *can't* let it happen. I hang the keys back on the hook, my mind racing. Grammy's saying something. I can see her moving into the kitchen. She wants me to sit down and keep talking.

But I have to do something. I have to act. Talk won't save him.

I'm out the door in less than a breath. I sprint up the street. I don't have a real plan. Not yet. Instinct carries me to the bus stop. Jeffrey was standing in this exact spot just this morning, thinking it would be another normal day.

My phone buzzes in my pocket. I slide it out enough to see Grammy's image looking at me. I don't have time to talk it through. Not if she doesn't want to help me. I shove the phone back down and try to make a plan. Maybe I could call an Uber? I'd have to lie about my age, though. And I'd have to use Mom's credit card on the app. Those consequences would be worth it, if it's what helps me save Jeffrey's life.

Looking around the neighborhood offers no inspiration. There are a few signs posted for missing cats. The mail carrier is working her way down the opposite end of the street. Two sweet-looking labs chase a ball in the park. No obvious solutions to my problem.

And then it hits me.

I don't need to go all the way to school. I can just go to the spot where it happens. I recognized that location in my vision. It's just outside our neighborhood. I can *walk* there.

My phone buzzes again, but I ignore it. I'm always going on walks with Grammy and Mom, so it's as easy as getting my bearings. Green Chapel Road. That's where I need to go. It's on the very far end of the neighborhood, past the house where Avery's parents used to live together. I start in that direction.

As I do, I retrace the details of the vision. Jeffrey looked like he was walking home from school. I can't help wondering if it's because he'll miss the bus? I know school lets out in an hour. It's not a ton of time, but more than enough for me to do *something*.

I begin walking, knowing I don't have a real plan for saving him yet. I have to do enough to make sure Jeffrey survives, but without being so weird that I get his attention. My mind races. Step one is actually pretty easy. I think back to the vision. What causes the accident?

The traffic cone.

One of the cones was jutting out too far into the street. The first car struck the cone and panicked. I can fix that. It takes fifteen minutes to navigate through the neighborhood backstreets and reach the spot where Green Chapel's speed limit slows a little for the downtown traffic. I'm thinking about how I'll identify the exact location my vision happened when I hear a screech of tires. Followed by a loud honk. There's a flicker in my vision. A glimpse of dark threads weaving through the air around me. And then I stumble back a step as a car comes literally inches from hitting me.

"Hey!"

I'm expecting Grammy, but it's not her. A high-school girl is staring at me like I've got three heads. All I can do is stare back, because she looks *so* familiar. She has light brown skin and wears a deep green gloss on her lips. Eye shadow to match. One strand of her dark, curled hair is dyed a lighter brown. I can't place where I know her from. Maybe she was in the vision?

"Try looking next time?" she shouts. "I almost hit you."

I can't believe I was about to cross the road without looking. She waves me across, and it looks like the same motion someone would make to shoo a mosquito. I wave an apology back and quickstep it across the street.

My adrenaline is pumping now. It might have been embarrassing, but it's also a good wake-up call. I'm not going to save Jeffrey by getting myself run over. Thankfully, the main road doesn't have a ton of traffic. It doesn't take long to find the right time to sprint across to the side of Green Chapel Road with the railroad tracks. There's a sidewalk running the length of the road, straight as an arrow, leading to another neighborhood in the distance. I put my back to downtown and start walking the other way.

It takes another five minutes for the cones to come into view.

I can see a few pieces of abandoned construction equipment ahead. They all circle a section of the road that's covered by one of those massive metal plates. I smile, remembering how Mom always screamed when Grammy sent us flying right over those kinds of bumps.

I keep walking past the area, because I didn't see any of this in my vision. It must be farther down the road. After a few minutes, I realize the cones go on forever. It doesn't help that the whole area kind of looks the same. All the trees are about the same height and color. The road has almost zero distinctive features. And the train tracks are train tracks.

Wonderful.

"I'll just have to move all of them." I circle back. I have to leave the safety of the sidewalk, but there's no traffic right now. I set my feet, take a deep breath, and give the first cone a huge shove. It goes flying. I let out a surprised laugh as it rolls. "Oops."

They're plastic and cheap. Surprisingly easy to move out of the way. It's not heavy lifting, but the work still takes time. I do my best to make sure every single cone is well clear of the road. Once or twice I think I've found the actual culprit from the vision. Each of them juts out so far into the road that I want to find the construction workers who set them here and ask what the heck they were thinking.

I'm almost done—just fifteen cones left—when a figure starts making their way up the sidewalk to me. I look up, distractedly nudging a cone aside with one foot, before realizing the person matches the cones. Well, not literally. It's a construction worker. He looks pretty young. Unruly hair juts out beneath an orange hard hat. He's jogging over, and I'm clearly his intended destination.

"Uhh ... Hello ... Could you not do that? I spent all morning setting those cones out!"

I can't believe my bad luck. He stops about fifteen feet away, chest still heaving. I can see construction vehicles making their way down the road. They're obviously about to do some kind of work here. My mind races. How much time do I have? And how do I explain this?

"Oh. Hi. Yes . . . I'm here with the Green . . . Homeowners' Association."

Isn't Grammy always talking about that? The guy does a double take.

"Aren't you like . . . a kid? Shouldn't you be in school?"

"I'm one of the youth representatives for the neighborhood. It's a volunteer position. Kind of like community service."

He frowns. "Okay. But what does this have to do with the cones?"

"Well, our neighborhood is right over there . . ."

I point to our distant neighborhood entrance. It's just a sign with some flowers on both sides. I'm mostly pointing at it to buy myself more time, because I have no idea what I could possibly say to him that would make any sense at all.

". . . and yeah. We were all very concerned. About these cones."

"The cones?" He looks even more confused. "But they're cones. We put them out here to keep people safe. We're installing cable lines up and down this entire sidewalk. It's a city requirement to have cones."

I pat the nearest cone, fully aware of how ridiculous I look.

"Well, they didn't meet our neighborhood's personal safety requirements. The neighborhood social media page was full of posts about them. Everyone said these cones are way too close to the road. Someone actually ran into one earlier today." I point back to the cone that I accidentally knocked over. "I was doing community service in the area and figured I'd come over and take care of things."

He gestures to the road. A few cars are passing.

"It's dangerous for you to be out here by yourself. Working on the side of the road? You're not even wearing a safety vest! Look. No offense, but they had me put those cones out that far for a reason. It's mandatory. I could get fired if they're not set out right. . . ."

All I can do is watch as he walks past me. Clearly, he's not convinced. I imagine him going back down the line and undoing all my hard work. Is this what Grammy meant about fate having its way? Even if I try to stop death, it will find a loophole? The guy has reached the first cone when I spot another figure approaching in the distance. Coming from the opposite direction.

"Jeffrey . . ."

My heart rate doubles. Jeffrey Johnson is patiently making his way up the road. I didn't realize how much time had passed. School must have let out already. I didn't finish. There are fifteen cones behind me. Did I get to the one that causes the accident? And what happens if this random construction worker puts out the cone that causes Jeffrey's death? I have to stop him. Desperate, I pull out a move from Mom's playbook and start dialing Grammy.

"Wait! I've got a senior representative of the Homeowners' Association on the line. She wants to make sure all this is . . . aboveboard."

I'm pretty sure that's something Mom would say. I've definitely heard her pull out the "Well, I'm going to bring in *this* person" line to motivate people she's working with on cases.

Sure enough, the construction worker stops in his tracks.

"Seriously? Wow. Okay. Hold on. Just let me get my boss."

He actually reaches for a walkie-talkie on his belt.

"Frank. Come in. We have an issue."

I can't believe it worked. There's a beep. Another voice cuts back. A few cars pass the spot, skirting the two of us carefully. It takes a second to realize none of this was in the vision. I wasn't here. Neither was this construction worker. Will those details change the future I saw? Did I do enough to save him? Jeffrey's close enough now to have spotted us.

"Copy that," the construction worker says. "Have it your way, kid. My boss is coming."

Across the road, Jeffrey keeps glancing over at me. I'm standing with a random construction worker, arguing about cones. I'm sure this looks pretty strange. Each step he takes feels like a strike of lightning. He keeps glancing down at his phone, and I have to fight the temptation to shout for him to run into the woods and get *away* from here. That wouldn't look suspicious at all. A few more cars pass.

And that's when I see the blue Subaru.

It's coming the opposite direction. Moving slower than it did in my vision. I stare as it approaches, ready to shout a warning, but when the second car in the vision appears, both of them come to a complete stop. A few construction workers are crossing the road. One of them must be Frank—the boss. The cars have slowed down to let them cross safely. Jeffrey Johnson passes the place where the car hit him in the vision. The arrival of three more construction workers has him even more curious. Thankfully, he keeps walking.

He's safe. He's actually safe.

"Celia?"

My own name summons me back. I realize Grammy's voice is chirping out from my phone. The construction workers are waiting. The boss crosses his arms. He's a big guy.

"What's the problem?" he asks. "We're *outside* your neighborhood, kid. I'm not sure who you've got on the phone there, but the Homeowners' Association doesn't get to make decisions about construction on public roads like this . . ."

Beyond them, Jeffrey has reached the front of our neighborhood. It's like he's passed into some kind of home-base area from the games we played as kids. Like no one can touch him now that he's in the imaginary safe zone. The construction workers are waiting for an answer. I lift the phone to my ear. Grammy's voice sounds instantly.

"Celia? What's happening? Who is there with . . ."

I've got one more act to pull off. I'll be able to answer her questions later.

"What's that, Grammy? I'm on the wrong road? Okay. Right. I'll let them know . . ."

I hear a clipped protest from her before hanging up. My heart is beating so fast. This is way outside my comfort zone. "Sorry about that," I say, shaking my head and putting on an innocent smile. "This was a mistake. I went to the wrong location. These cones look great!"

I get out of there as fast as I safely can. A car passes, and then when the road clears, I cross. I can almost feel the construction workers staring at me, wondering what on earth just happened. But when I reach the front of my neighborhood, a wave of euphoria sweeps through me.

About two hundred yards ahead, Jeffrey is walking. He

looks so very alive. I actually did it. My heart is still hammering in my chest. I saved someone's life. I keep my distance, watching Jeffrey Johnson trudge up the street like the miracle that he is.

At the top of the hill, he pauses and glances back. A shiver runs down my spine. He's tall for a seventh grader. I've never heard him say a word. He thumbs the cleats dangling over one shoulder, and it seems like he's looking right at me. For a second, I think he's going to shout something. Instead, he turns and keeps walking.

My phone rings again. It's Grammy. I can barely press the accept button before her voice comes flying out. "I predict that you've got a *lot* of explaining to do."

I can't help smiling. She might be mad, but I feel more useful than I've felt in my entire life. The words come breathlessly through my lips.

"I saved him, Grammy. I actually *saved* him."

CHAPTER FOUR

Second Sight(ing)

I make sure to take a different direction home than Jeffrey. The last thing I need is for him to think that I'm stalking him through the neighborhood or something. It's weird, though. I just saved his life, and we've never really talked before. I'm not sure what the protocol is for heroically saving someone who doesn't know I saved them. Do I introduce myself?

Hey, I just saved your life. You get to go to college and eat bacon cheeseburgers and live a full life now. You're very welcome. What's that? You want to thank me? A gift card? Perfect!

The excitement doesn't completely take away the guilt of how I saved him. Lying to a construction worker wasn't exactly how I wanted to kick off my career as a seer. I'm pretty sure my lawyer of a mother wouldn't approve. But the guilt can't quite match the excitement. Jeffrey Johnson is about to arrive at his home. He'll hug his mom when he gets there. Do his homework.

It's so strange and wonderful to know I'm the reason he's alive.

I'm passing the doggie-bag dispenser at the corner of the park when an unexpected scent curls to life. Not fertilizer or dog business or blooming flowers. My stomach drops.

It's the smell of a campfire.

"Wait," I whisper. "No, no, no . . ."

And my view of the neighborhood vanishes. Color sketches back to life, and I'm standing at the very center of our school's basketball court. Right on top of our Patriot mascot's cartoon musket. I look up and—with sudden and complete terror—realize the entire school is staring directly at me. My heart hammers in my chest. What is happening? Why am I down here? Is this a nightmare?

I'm saved by the voice of Principal Locklear. Of course. An end-of-day assembly.

"We're going to dismiss buses four, seven, nine, twelve, and eighteen."

My eyes search the crowd as different rows come to life and start to move.

I'm not really sure why I'm seeing this vision . . .

. . . but there he is.

On the very top row of the gymnasium bleachers: Jeffrey Johnson. Our bus number was called, so he's walking down one of the rows with his friends. The guys behind him are shoving and laughing, just having fun. It's not hard to see the effect on the whole row as they make their way to the exit. Jeffrey adjusts his bag to get by the girl at the end of the row right as someone comes stumbling from behind. Their hands shove out. Jeffrey's caught off-balance.

I watch as he goes flying into the hip-high barrier at the top of the bleachers.

A scream sounds. The bars unhinge. Jeffrey starts to fall.

My vision stutters, blinking back to the park. I'm on the ground, heaving and struggling to breathe. Grammy's not there to coach me through it this time. No one is. It takes a solid minute to get my breathing back to normal.

I sprint the rest of the way home. Grammy's car is still the only one in the garage. Mom must not be home from work yet. I come barreling inside. Grammy is waiting in the kitchen. She has a knowing look on her face. "Let me guess," she says. "You saw another death."

I stare at her and ask the one question no one should ever ask a seer.

"How'd you know?"

She sets a hand on an ancient-looking book and slides it halfway across the table.

"It's time to teach you the rules."

CHAPTER FIVE

Homework

W hat is that smell?"

Grammy sniffs dramatically. "Tradition."

The front cover of the ancient book reads: *The Cleary Family Guide Book*. I always thought it was an old photo album. In fact, I'm pretty sure the one time I flipped it open, there *were* a bunch of Polaroid pictures inside. I'm not sure if my memory is off or if that was some kind of protective magical spell. Knowing Grammy, either one is a possibility.

It's an actual *guide* to using our magic.

Like those video-game guides that teach you how to fight the final boss or something. I turn the pages, and the smell of more "tradition" wafts into the air. It is kind of cool. Except for the fact that the contents are completely confusing.

The original author's descriptions are easy to follow. The problem is that dozens of other people have scribbled notes and corrections all through the margins. There are different colors and fonts. Varying degrees of sanity. Even a few doodles. Grammy sees me looking a little lost and decides to intervene. She guides me back to an earlier section and double-taps a specific page.

"Read all of this."

There's a particularly helpful chart that breaks down everything.

"So . . . there are two types of seers?"

Grammy nods. "Catalysts and Witnesses."

After those two words, I spot the word *Specializations* written. There are seven categories listing over twenty different types of seers. There's a note pointing out that each of these specializations can have even *deeper* specializations.

❁ THE CLEARY FAMILY GUIDE BOOK ❁

∾∾∾ SPECIALIZATIONS ∾∾∾

LUCK
Charmist
Lurebird
Chanceling

PHYSICAL
Psychometrist
Tactile Engineer
Two-Steps

MENTAL
Precognition Engineer
Clairvoyants
Auras

ASTROLOGY
Wonderers
Wanderers

DREAM
Dreamwalker
Manipulator

DEATH
Grimdark
Doomspeak
Deathwell

SYMBOLIC
Arcana
Relics
Mediums
Wheel Breakers

I'm pretty sure everything listed comes from our family's past. At some point, there was a seer in our family who possessed the powers described. That's confirmed by another note that mentions there might be undiscovered categories.

"Okay . . . so which one am I?"

"Most likely you are a Witness," Grammy replies. "Almost all of us are. A Catalyst is someone who *creates* the future. There have been very few in our family tree. Generally, they see a distant vision and spend their entire lives trying to create that future with their actions and words. It is a future that could not exist without them."

I frown. "But I'm not one of those? I'm a Witness?"

"The most common branch," Grammy confirms. "You saw a glimpse of a *potential* future. The vision of the car crash would have happened if you had not stopped it. Witness gifts all manifest in different ways. As you know, my preferred branch of magic is *psychometry*."

I nod confidently. We've talked about this one before.

"Visions glimpsed through specific items."

Grammy smiles. "Correct. Your cousin Martha reads

auras. That's in the Mental category. And your cousin Mary is a Chanceling. She sees probabilities. The vision you saw? Imagine seeing seventeen of them, all in a flash."

Just thinking about that makes me dizzy. "No thanks. What's my specialty?"

Grammy licks a finger, flipping the pages again, and stops almost exactly in the middle of the book. "It's hard to tell this early, but we could make a few educated guesses. Maybe a Deathwell or a Grimdark? Both are . . . specifically related to death prophecies. But it's also possible you're a Precognition Engineer. The vision you described was incredibly specific. It sounds as if you were able to move around inside the vision, watching it in real time. That level of control is usually connected to precognitions and clairvoyants."

My head is spinning again. "What's the difference between them?"

"One has more vowels."

"Very funny."

Grammy sees my expression and sighs. "You're right. I'm sorry, dear. This is a *lot*. And we haven't even gotten into how some of the branches combine. Not every seer fits perfectly into just one branch of magic. I was hoping you'd have an easier first go at this, but sometimes fate deals us a difficult hand. Let's talk about death."

She turns the pages again, opening up a chapter I've already read. She assigns me to read it one more time for good measure. The problem is that none of the voices agree on anything. Especially not on how prophecy and death work. One note disagrees with the original author, but the next note rants about how wrong the first note-writer was. Each paragraph is like wading through a swamp, and it doesn't take long for my mental shoes to feel stuck in the mud.

Eventually I look up at Grammy. "So ... there are no rules?"

Her eyes widen. "Of course there are rules!"

"But none of these people agree on anything! How can there be rules if they all believe different things about the rules?"

"Here." She drags her chair over so we're sitting side by side. "Rule number one."

I read it out loud. *"It is well known that everyone dies."*

"Hard to argue with that." She traces her finger down. "And rule number two."

"Fate is persistent. It will not give up its quarry."

She leans back in her chair. "Those are the rules, Celia. We know that people die. We know that fate chooses. Death can be delayed but not undone. I am so very proud of what you did today. I expected no less. You have such a good heart, but even a good heart cannot stop death. Every time you save Jeffrey, a new vision will follow of a new death. It will go on like that forever, until death finally has its way."

I don't know what to say to that. I'm old enough to understand that everyone dies, but something about the way she's describing things makes it feel so *hopeless*. I'm still sitting there, thinking about it, when her seat creaks. She crosses to the kitchen and starts making tea, like this is all stressing her out. Never mind that I'm the one who just found out I'm in the boxing ring against death. I inherited my mother's stubbornness, though, which has me pulling the book to my chest to read the section on death a third time.

There are several different specializations in the death-prediction community. One branch is called Doomspeaks. Powerful, old-school prophets that warn entire societies about what's coming. They're the ones who raise a red flag before the local volcano explodes.

The second group is known as Grimdarks. They sound more like the classic Grim Reaper character in movies and books. They receive a vision of someone who is about to die and are tasked with being nearby at the moment of their death. Something about their magic—or their presence—eases the person's path into the next world.

And the last category is called a Deathwell. I like them the most. Their job is to save a subject until they can die a *good* death. The text argues that such deaths bring hope to the rest of humanity. Accidental car crashes are sad. Jumping in front of a bullet to save someone? Inspiring.

In a very twisted way, that makes sense.

But as I read back through the categories, I start to feel hopeless again. Grammy is right. None of the branches save people. A seer announces doom or prepares souls or improves the quality of the death. There's not a single word about how to stop a death permanently.

There is one section about trading prophecies. That has me excited for exactly two minutes. I'm wondering if maybe it means I can trade Jeffrey's death prophecy for a better one—like one where he wins the lottery or scores a game-winning goal. But it becomes clear that it's not that kind of trade. It says the vision can be given or taken by another seer. It doesn't stop the person from dying. Just makes saving the victim someone else's job.

I groan. "This is the worst."

There are a few transitions between pages that don't even make sense. It's like the writer forgot the topic they were talking about and skipped right on to something else. Almost an hour passes before I push away from the desk, eyes so tired they're starting to cross.

Grammy is there. She sets a cup of tea down. "And? What did you learn?"

"Jeffrey is going to die."

She nods gravely.

"Unless I save him."

Her eyes shut. "Celia. You'd have to save him for the rest of his life."

"Then that's what I'll do."

Grammy looks briefly frustrated, which makes me even angrier.

"What's the point?" I ask. "If we can't make a difference?"

"A seer provides clarity." It's a line I've heard her say hundreds of times. "We inform. We instruct. We encourage. It's our job to bring out the best possible future in this one, wonderful life."

"Except for Jeffrey's best future? It's not fair."

"It rarely is," she whispers. "But there are more beautiful things in this life than *fair*."

A second later, we both hear the garage rumble open. Mom is home. I panic a little at the thought of trying to explain all this to her. Even though Grammy and I are in the middle of an argument, it doesn't stop me from looking her way for advice now.

"What do I say?"

47

"Don't lie to her," Grammy advises. "But don't tell her the truth."

I shake my head. "You're like a walking sphinx."

"Then you're lucky I haven't eaten you. I would never suggest actually lying to your mother, Celia. Right now, she is having a strange day. Nearly as strange as yours. Her daughter has stepped into a world where she cannot set foot. There's so much unknown. It's frightening for her. I suggest sharing a few details without overwhelming her. I'd like to think your mother is strong enough to take all this in. She's an incredible, accomplished woman. But my mother was strong too, and she never adjusted to the fact that I had magic and she did not. Trust me, your mother won't ask about the details."

Somehow that makes me feel worse.

"Are you sure?"

"I am. Drink your tea."

Grammy tidies the kitchen as Mom backs through the door. She's got her phone pinched against one shoulder. "I know. That's the way he wanted to do it. Beats me. Hey. Gotta go."

She tosses the phone into her purse and smiles my way. Her heels all but melt off her feet as she crosses the room and slides an unmarked white box across the table to me. I've always *loved* this about Mom. Even if she ducked out on me today—and even if that hurt a lot—she's always left her work at the office. When she's home with us, she's home.

"Consider this a peace offering. I'm sorry I had to miss your big day, honey. These are fresh from Utica Bakery. Want to eat some doughnuts and watch that werewolf show?!"

That has me laughing. "Vampires, Mom. It's in the title of the show. *Vampire High.*"

"I hate that show," Grammy pipes in. "It's so unrealistic."

Mom catches my eye and we both grin. Grammy's always been opposed to the *flashier* magical entities. She feels prophets and seers are woefully underrepresented in pop culture.

"To the couch!" Mom orders. "Ma, you want in on the doughnut draft?"

"I'm not a heathen," she answers. "Doughnuts for dinner?"

Mom and I share another grin as I escort the doughnuts

to the living room. I flip the lid, eyeing the glazed treats before plopping onto the couch. Mom sits down too close to me and grabs me when I try to squirm away. I laugh before settling my head against her shoulder. She kisses me quick on the forehead and then looks around.

"Oh no," she groans. "Is the remote on your side of the couch?"

Before I can glance over, the TV turns on. We both look back. Grammy is settling in at the kitchen table, remote in hand. "At your service," she calls. "How do I activate the Netflix?"

Mom laughs, and her laughter shakes into my body and has me laughing. Before long we're both cracking up. Grammy accidentally turns on some scandalous-looking soap opera, and we double over again. It takes a while to catch our breath.

For as long as I can remember, this is what our life was like.

I always got the best of both worlds. There's Grammy with her otherworldly wisdom. I've always loved the way she can make a walk down the greenway feel like a stroll through Narnia. Mom is the opposite. She's so firmly rooted in the real world. She runs a book club and goes to concerts and lives life like normal people do. For as long as I can remember, I got to float between *both* worlds. An image of Jeffrey falling from the bleachers whispers into my mind.

My perfect little worlds aren't ever going to be the same.

Mom nudges my shoulder. "You okay?"

I nod back. "Just hungry. Let the draft begin!"

Drafts are one of our things. About five years ago, Mom joined some fantasy football league. She got such an adrenaline rush from it that she started randomly declaring imaginary drafts. Favorite pizza places. Colors. Cereals. Our doughnut drafts are always intense.

"With the first pick in the draft," I say dramatically. "I'll take the maple-bacon."

"Of course you will. Team Law School will select the chocolate cream–filled doughnut."

As Grammy struggles to get *Vampire High* loaded up,

Mom and I trade picks back and forth. At the end, we collect our spoils and start our unhealthy dinner. Grammy actually manages to get us to the right screen. Mom takes a second while the show is loading to lean closer to me.

"Did it go well?"

I can't help smiling. I know she cares. I know how hard it must be to feel like she's on the outside of this. Grammy's advice echoes: *Don't lie to her, but don't tell her the truth*. Today really wasn't what I thought it would be. I thought I'd be celebrating. I'm mostly just frustrated by the idea that I can't permanently save Jeffrey's life. But there was that moment—walking back into our neighborhood—when my heart pounded with pride at saving him. That part felt kind of good.

"It was great."

She kisses my forehead again. Grammy was right. She doesn't want the details. Maybe it hurts too much to know them, but she cares enough to ask how it went. I love her for that.

"Hey!" Mom bolts upright. "You watched the show without me!"

My eyes flick to the screen. We stopped a few nights ago after watching the Season 3 finale, but there's a red bar on the screen that shows someone watched two episodes of Season 4.

"I didn't watch it! I swear!"

After a few seconds, we both look back at Grammy.

"Well," she says. "I wanted to see if Sullivan survived. . . ."

And the Cleary home fills with laughter again.

CHAPTER SIX

The Courtyard Kids

E arth to Cleary! Come in, Cleary! The movement needs you. Over."

Sophie snaps her fingers in my face. I blink distractedly and realize we're walking through one of the locker bays. If anyone else snapped their fingers an inch from my nose, I'd probably be annoyed. But Sophie exists to be in people's faces. It's a defining characteristic of her friendship. And a big part of what I love about her.

I must have zoned out. It's happened all morning. All I can think about is Jeffrey Johnson.

"What were you saying?"

Sophie's expression is the definition of impatience. "I was talking about *your* rights. About you and the legacy of all the women who have come before you. The fight, Cleary, the fight!"

I nod back to her. "What petition are you running this week?"

Sophie believes the world can be changed for the better. Her mom has been a big-time activist since the '90s, and Sophie inherited the same trademark enthusiasm. She is somehow both the most exhausting and admirable person I've ever met. She's also one of only two friends I have left after Avery decided she was too cool to hang out with "The Courtyard Kids."

"Our field trip to Jungle Rapids." Sophie reaches out and taps a form I didn't even realize I was holding in my hand. "It's in the small print. Inequality is always in the small print. We have a dress code, and there's not a single word about what the boys have to wear. There's no way we're letting them get away with this!"

I nod to her as we make our way into the courtyard. It's a Tuesday, which is when a lot of clubs meet, so the courtyard traffic is lighter than usual. There are always four or five groups weaving in and out of each other out here. We've all accepted one fact about ourselves: we are weird. There's a group that always wears cat hats and another that talks about their favorite MMORPGs and one that argues politics.

When I was in sixth grade and she was in seventh, Avery brought me here for the first time. The courtyard had been her safe haven the year before, and it quickly became the one place at school where I really felt at home. Even after she abandoned us, it still feels that way.

DeSean sits at our normal table. He's wearing thick-framed glasses and a fresh mustard stain on his collar. As we arrive, he's taking a dramatic picture of his half-eaten turkey sandwich.

"What's on the menu today, D?"

He scrolls through filters before looking up. "I call it the Turkatron."

Sophie and I take our seats, eyeing his monstrosity of a

sandwich. Even after he's taken a few bites out of the thing, it looks about the size of an actual turkey. Sophie removes a fork from her own lunch box and prods the towering sandwich. "That thing still has a pulse."

"It's not as bad as his Steakenstein Sandwich," I point out.

Sophie nods at the memory. "Oh yeah. That one got back up and ran away."

We laugh as DeSean rolls his eyes. He's focused on perfecting his latest Instagram post. I unpack my own lunch, scanning the rest of the courtyard. Naturally, Jeffrey Johnson isn't here. I've been looking around for him in classes, too, even though I know he's not in any of mine.

"Just need a good caption," DeSean says. "How about . . . 'Turkatron: You're gonna need a siesta'? Or do you think that's too focused on my fan base in Spain?"

Sophie's eyes widen. "You have followers in Spain?"

"Tons of them," he answers, still typing. "But I'm *really* big in the Czech Republic."

Sophie stares at her own peanut butter sandwich and shakes her head. I pluck a grape from my lunch box, hiding a smile. Sophie spends every waking hour trying to change the world. I know it annoys her sometimes that DeSean has a huge platform that is focused on gourmet sandwiches. Their arguments are epic.

I watch them go back and forth, and another little knot forms in my stomach. I wish I could tell them about Jeffrey Johnson and my first vision. It'd be nice to talk to someone besides Grammy about everything. But the last time someone found out about my family's magic, it didn't go so well. Avery called my grandmother fake. Then she said I was a freak for believing her. She stopped returning my texts and showed up to school with a new group of friends.

"Earth to Celia," DeSean says. "What do you think?"

I blink. "About what?"

"Me going to the Czech Republic," he says.

I clearly missed the conversation. "I hear it's nice this time of year?"

DeSean throws that back at Sophie, who groans at me like the world is ending. As the conversation starts to spin in a new direction, I remember lunch is my last free period. If I want to make sure I get to the gym before Jeffrey's accident, I need to go now.

I don't have a great plan. I guess I could just stand at the end of the row of bleachers? Make sure he doesn't fall when he gets pushed? But the more I think about trying to save him that way, the messier it sounds. If Grammy is right, I'm going to have to save Jeffrey a billion times. He'll probably get super weirded out if he keeps almost dying and I'm always the one who saves him.

Determined, I grab my book bag and stand.

"Leaving already, Celia?" DeSean asks.

"Forgot to turn in some homework. See you guys later."

The two of them wave goodbye, and I head straight for the gym. Our school does this thing the administrators call "ALL Lunch." Every student eats at the exact same time, which means every locker bay is full of conversations and half-huddled groups and loud laughter.

I'm halfway to the gym when a group of soccer players comes bustling past me, most of them wearing bright red hoodies with their team names printed on the front. I almost faint when I spot Jeffrey at the back of their group.

Most of the boys bustle past without a glance. But Jeffrey's eyes lock onto mine. I blush a little. I forgot how things like eye contact can be so awkward. It gets worse, though, when he stops dead in his tracks and nods to me. I raise my hand in an uncomfortable, childish wave.

"Hey!" he says.

I stare at him. He's talking to me. I've never even heard him speak.

"Hi." I finally realize the wave thing is awkward and lower my hand. "It's Jeffrey, right?"

His name is literally on the front of his hoodie. He smiles and taps the etching.

"Good guess. Celia?"

I nod back. "Cleary. Celia Cleary."

Some of the soccer crew has whipped around the corner and left him behind. But there are a few of them lingering and looking back at us like they're studying a strange zoo exhibit. I can feel the heat creeping up my neck as Jeffrey speaks.

"Were you in trouble or something?"

"In trouble?"

"Yesterday," he says. "You were over near that construction site? Those guys looked pretty upset. I don't know. I was just making sure everything was cool."

Of course. Seeing me surrounded by construction workers probably looked super weird.

"Oh yeah! It was a misunderstanding."

He nods now and realizes people are waiting for him. "Good. Glad you're okay."

And he starts walking away. My heart hammers in my chest as I start walking the other direction. *Glad you're okay?* I almost laugh. I'm the one who saved him. *Glad you're okay.* I glance back in time to see him vanish around a corner, and I can't help smiling. He's actually kind of nice. I wasn't expecting that. Which also has me realizing that I don't really know *anything* about him.

Note to self: do some research.

I arrive on the south side of our massive gym, peeking through the double doors. There's a game of pickup basketball happening. A teacher is monitoring things from the far end of the room, but I can see him glancing at his phone every few seconds. Two steps into the room and I notice my first obstacle.

"Great," I mutter. "The bleachers aren't out."

I was hoping to point out the loose railing casually, but when they're folded up? There's no way I could casually see anything. My eyes roam back to the teacher. Maybe they'll pull them down after lunch or something? Biting my lip in thought, I decide to cross the room. Saving Jeffrey is forcing me to talk to far more people than I'd like.

"Excuse me! Sorry."

The teacher glances up from his phone.

"When will they pull out the bleachers for the school assembly?"

He raises an eyebrow. "Not until Friday. Which is the actual day of the assembly."

"Oh yeah. Of course. Thanks."

I start walking back through the gym. *Of course.* I can't believe I didn't piece that together on my own. We only have school assemblies on Fridays. I assumed it was today because I thought the vision would always happen in sequence. It's kind of perfect, really. Plenty of extra time to make sure that I have a plan in place to save Jeffrey.

But then I realize something else. Something very important.

He doesn't die every day.

This new discovery comes with its own set of consequences, both good and bad. The first obvious one is that I get to take some days off. It's kind of nice knowing this isn't a full-time gig.

But it also means I won't know which day he's supposed to die. It'll be a guessing game. Really, it was pure luck that I saw him bite the dust during an assembly. Those are always on Fridays. I should have been able to figure it out on my own. But what about the car crash from my first vision? Or other random events? It's going to be really hard to figure out *when* each one will happen.

The bell rings.

I've got math class next. I start heading that way, and

for the first time, math seems like an easy alternative. Grammy's spent the last few years teaching me about the responsibilities and the privileges of being a seer. I always imagined I'd be sitting in our townhome, reading people's palms or something.

No one told me so much walking and talking would be involved.

It's been two days and I already need a nap.

CHAPTER SEVEN

Awkward

I don't need prophetic visions to know the bus ride home will be awkward. It's always awkward now. Back in sixth grade, I used to look forward to taking the bus. Avery and I would jam into a seat near the front. Shoulders pressed together, we'd play video games or talk about our favorite comic books. Even on the bad days—when I was feeling sick or when Avery's parents had a huge argument—we'd sit there, shoulder to shoulder, facing the world together.

Now I make my way to a very strategic and lonely seat

in the middle of the bus. Not far enough up front that I'll be sitting with the sixth graders. But not so far back that I have to listen to the sound of Avery flirting with Jordan Lyles.

Let's just say that last summer a lot happened.

I knew Avery's mom and dad were having a hard time. It was all Avery talked about. One night, I mentioned that Grammy is kind of an advisor. It's always hard to use words like *seer* or *psychic* or *prophet*. People usually think it's a joke. But Avery's mom was curious. I didn't think much of it at the time, but apparently, she visited Grammy a few days later.

A week after that, Avery's parents split up. I have no idea what Grammy told her—and she'd never tell me even if I asked—but that was the beginning of the end. Avery started acting really weird around me, and when I told her she was acting weird, she said my whole family was *weird*.

It was the way she said it, though. Like *weird* was a curse word. She mentioned Grammy's business and accused her of being a fake. Which got me all kinds of mad. I told her she was wrong, and she said I was a freak if I believed in stuff like that.

We were both so upset that we didn't talk the next day.

And the next one.

And then Avery randomly decided to go to cheerleading camp (she'd always loved gymnastics, but I'd never heard her say anything nice about the cheerleading team). When the new school year started, she decided our friendship was over. She stopped coming to the courtyard. She started dating Jordan Lyles. She had new friends to sit with at lunch. All because I tried to help her mom out.

Now every bus ride home is a reminder that nothing is the same.

I shove into the tenth seat from the front and stare out the window as our bus navigates through the first neighborhood stops. I watch trees whip by, and the sun flickers through the branches. For a while, the landscape just melts across the window and I don't think about anything.

But a throat clears, and I look up to find Jeffrey Johnson sitting right across the aisle from me. The first thing I do is frown at him, because he usually sits in the back with everyone else. He notices me noticing him and tugs out one of his earbuds. "What?"

I stare back at him. "I didn't say anything."

"Oh. Sorry." He licks his lips, and I can tell he's thinking about saying something else. I can't help noticing one of the Kapowski sisters turning back to look at us. She whips back to her twin sister and whispers something. Her reaction has me realizing something I've kind of been ignoring.

Jeffrey Johnson is really cute.

He's got short hair that crests up naturally in the front. His skin is a light olive shade and his eyes are bright brown. I've never really thought about him being cute until now.

"What'd you say?"

My eyes widen. Did I say that out loud?

"What's cute?" he asks.

"Boots," I say, recovering quickly. His soccer cleats are dangling from his bag like they always are. I make an exaggerated show of pointing at them. "I said nice boots."

He shakes his head. "Oh. Sorry. Yeah. They're the Tessa-X 90s."

"So you really like . . . sportsball."

He laughs, and the sound is almost as surprising as the fact that he's talking to me.

"Soccer. I like soccer."

My stomach feels like it's tied in a thousand knots. Random ideas are flinging themselves into the front of my brain. I do my best to pick something that makes sense.

"My mom likes football. She plays fantasy football every year."

"Oh. That's pretty cool."

Jeffrey smiles awkwardly and it finally hits me. The boy I'm supposed to save—might be stuck saving forever—is talking to me. Getting to know him feels like dangerous territory. I can almost hear Grammy's warning voice in the back of my head. But he doesn't know I'm saving his life, so I just keep talking like all this is super normal.

"It's not really my thing. In fact, there's one day every year in July where there's no sportsball. My grammy and I celebrate it. We throw a cookout and everything."

"It's not that bad! Have you ever *been* to a soccer game?" He taps his cleats like they're capable of teleporting us to one. "You'd change your mind if you saw one in person."

"Is that an invitation to watch the Peak City Patriots?"

He snorts a laugh. Usually Grammy is the only one who laughs at my jokes.

"Not our team," he says. "I mean, we're pretty good. I was talking about a big game. Last year my dad took me and my little brother on a trip to England. I watched Tottenham play at Wembley. The Spurs won. It was amazing."

I nod sagely. "Yes. The Spurs. I was telling someone how much I love the . . . Spurs."

He laughs again. "I'm just saying you should give it a chance."

I'm trying to think of something funny to say when the bus gasps to a stop. I look up from our conversation like a startled bird and realize we're already home. How'd we get here so fast? I glance back at Jeffrey, but he's busy throwing his bag over one shoulder. His water bottle fell down under the seat. I watch as he performs some relatively complicated gymnastics to retrieve it.

I'm waiting for him—and I realize I actually want to keep talking to him.

But just a few rows back, Avery is uncurling from Jordan Lyles and collecting her backpack. I know in a few seconds she'll turn around and start walking up the aisle. The thought of her locking eyes with me is so uncomfortable that I'm already turning red.

It's easier to leave.

Before Jeffrey can resurface, I bolt for the front. Down the stairs and out into waiting sunlight. Birds are darting between trees overhead. I feel guilty abandoning him in the middle of a conversation, but that doesn't stop my feet from marching down the road as fast as possible, back into the safety of our townhome. It takes a few seconds for all the feelings I have about Avery to fade away.

My mind returns to Jeffrey. It's kind of amazing, really. In five minutes, I learned more about him than I've learned in the last five years.

He's been to London.

He loves soccer. A lot.

He has a little brother.

I can hear Grammy calling my name from the kitchen, but I stand with my back to the closed front door for a second longer. I smile as I remember the last thing I learned about Jeffrey Johnson. For some strange reason, he thinks I'm funny.

I'm still smiling as I walk into the kitchen.

CHAPTER EIGHT

(Un)Prepared

For three straight nights, I dream the vision of Jeffrey falling at the assembly. Grammy nods when I mention the repetitions at breakfast.

"It's all you ever think about. Of course you're dreaming it."

It probably doesn't help that I've been reading through the guide book every night before bed. Instead of finding answers, I just keep coming away with more questions.

"So let's say I save Jeffrey. . . ."

Grammy offers me a skeptical look but says nothing.

"What happens next? Would I see visions of other people?"

She nods. "I believe so. That is how it normally works. Although, how your visions arrive is another matter. Some seers require touch. Others sense futures near them. There are even some seers who are given visions of particularly important events in their time period."

And now for the harder question.

"I was reading last night that your first vision is a sign of what you'll always see. Kind of like a flavor." That was the word the book had used. "Does that mean I'll always see death?"

Grammy stops stirring her tea, a pained expression on her face. It's clear she didn't expect me to arrive at that conclusion so quickly. Maybe she was waiting to tell me.

"It might," she admits. "There is some science behind first visions being a *foundational* clue to a seer's magic. It might mean you'll see other deaths. But it might also mean some other category we can't recognize yet. We cannot know until . . ."

She trails off and I finish the sentence for her. I finish it with what *I* want to happen.

"Until I save Jeffrey."

Mom bustles into the room, cutting off any attempt Grammy might make to change my mind. The two of them start talking about an entirely different topic. My mind wades through what Grammy just told me. The idea that I might be stuck dealing with death forever is not comforting.

"Celia?" Mom asks.

I glance up. "Yeah?"

"I was asking what your favorite flavor is at the Grazing Goat. I can never remember what it's called. . . ."

She's watching me expectantly, and it's clear I blanked on more than just one question. Across the table, Grammy's throwing me a worried look. I smile at Mom.

"It's the Cinnamon Caramel Oatmeal Cookie," I answer. "Some of their specials are really good too, though. Why? Are we going out there sometime soon?"

Mom gestures to the colorful calendar hanging on our pantry door. "At the end of the month, remember? The Pimiento Cheese Festival is in that big field right across the street. I figured we'd start with savory and then head there for sweet. Didn't you want to go? You spent an entire Saturday morning showing me pictures of grilled cheeses from the last festival."

"Oh yeah! DeSean told me about it. I definitely want to go."

Mom stands up and ferries her cereal bowl to the sink. "You know, I'm off work early today. If you're up for a little drive, I could pull you out of school. We could head out that way and do some shopping. The Grazing Goat is surrounded by all those fancy boutiques. Someone's birthday is coming up."

She nods in Grammy's direction, but my mind is stuck on the other part of her sentence. Alarm bells are ringing in my head. The threat of her pulling me out of school on today of all days.

"No!" The word comes out a little too forcefully. "Sorry. There's an assembly today. I think there's supposed to be some guest speaker or something. I wanted to hear it."

Mom shrugs as she picks up her briefcase. "No worries. Have a good day, honey. I'm going to make a grocery run, so don't forget to text me if you want anything."

She sweeps in to kiss my forehead before heading out. The face Grammy is giving me could be in the dictionary next to the word *disapproval*. Maybe I should feel guilty for turning Mom's offer down, but I really don't. This is a matter of life and death. I know I'm doing the right thing.

As the garage door closes, Grammy takes her own plate to the sink. I can tell she's searching for the right words. But she turns back around and sweeps in for a kiss of her own.

"Have a good day, dear. My first appointment will be here soon. These futures won't tell themselves. . . ."

No words of warning? I watch her disappear into the living room and can't help feeling a little suspicious. Either she's accepted the fact that I'm not giving up, or she knows something I don't. I take a deep breath, grab my book bag, and head out the front door.

Jeffrey Johnson's not at the bus stop today. I've definitely seen his parents drive him to school a few times, so it's not abnormal or anything. Avery's there, though, flipping through pictures on her phone. She glances up long enough to realize it's me, then stares back at her phone like the secrets of the universe are being revealed there. Thankfully, the bus whips around the corner a few seconds later.

The school day moves slower than normal. Lunch finally rolls around, and I feel like one of those bugs that's been trapped in prehistoric amber for centuries. Instead of heading for the courtyard, I check on the gymnasium first. A quick glance shows that the bleachers *still* aren't out. It's kind of hard to ask someone to fix the railing if it's folded up with everything else.

I grind my teeth and head back to the courtyard. I could always just sit at the end of the row and make sure Jeffrey doesn't fall? But what if a teacher asks me to keep moving and forces me to walk down before he arrives? It's also possible that I'd have a hard time actually catching him. He's bigger than I am. We might end up just falling together.

Besides, it will be better if I can save him and stay off his radar for now. I have a feeling there's a *lot* of rescuing in my future. The final period before assembly arrives.

My social studies teacher—Mrs. Honea—stands in front of everyone. I distantly hear her walking the rest of the class through today's schedule. Only when the entire class groans in unison do I snap out of my daydream. "It wouldn't be a pop quiz without the pop," Mrs. Honea is saying. "Clear your desks."

The rest of the class is still groaning. Folders vanish. Zippers sound. I stare up at the board and remember we were supposed to read an article about the Cold War last night. My heart's beating a little faster in my chest as Mrs. Honea makes her way around the room and distributes her dreaded half-sheets to each student. Panicked, I glance back at DeSean.

"Who's in the Cold War again?" I whisper.

He stares at me. "You serious?"

"Come on, DeSean."

"Russia," he whispers. "But I have a feeling that's not going to get you too far, Cleary."

We both go quiet as Mrs. Honea starts working her way down our row. I can already hear pencils scratching across papers on the other side of the room. This is not going to go well.

A quiz lands on my desk. I stare at the first question.

Name two of the nations that were a part of the Warsaw Pact.

I scribble down Russia, but I have zero clue about the other ones. And I know that Mrs. Honea likes to start her quizzes with easy questions. So the next three on the sheet will be even harder. Great. I work on the one other thing I feel confident about. In careful letters, I write my name at the top of the page. Mrs. Honea gives ten points for getting that basic information correct. Unfortunately, that's about as far as I get. The other questions might as well be written in Russian.

It takes about two seconds for my mind to wander back to today's *real* problem: Jeffrey Johnson. There's just thirty minutes left in this period. I'm running out of time. So I flip my quiz facedown, remove a small handbag from my backpack, and head up to Mrs. Honea's desk.

She sees me coming and raises a questioning eyebrow.

"Bathroom?" I pair the whispered question with a little shake of the handbag. Avery taught me this last year. Any time a teacher thinks you're going to the bathroom for a specific reason, they're always more likely to let you go.

"Are you done with your quiz?" she whispers back.

I picture the blank spaces below each question. "All done."

She nods and hands me a clipboard. "Take the hall pass."

A few classmates look up as I cross the room and slip out. The hallways are empty. I ignore the bathroom on my right and head left instead. My stomach flutters nervously. I've never gone anywhere I'm not *supposed* to go, but the only teacher I see smiles at me before going into a teachers' lounge. I guess these are the perks of being a good student.

I turn down the next hallway and find the gymnasium's double doors waiting for me. A quick glance through the thin paneled window shows the bleachers are out. "Finally."

The place looks empty. The gym classes must be outside for this period. It takes a little courage, but I push my way inside and head straight for the far end of the room. I've seen the faulty railing four times now. I know exactly which section of the bleachers it's on.

I reach into the handbag. There's only one item inside, and it's not what Mrs. Honea would have guessed. It's the one item I knew how to use that might be useful: duct tape.

Right as I reach the end of the bleachers, I hear a rattle in the opposite corner. I jump a little bit, but look back to see the maintenance closet is open. Mr. Simms is shuffling items in and out.

If there's ever any problem in the school, teachers and students know to go to Mr. Simms. He wears a Patriots school T-shirt from a few years ago, tucked into a pair of jeans that have seen better days. He's also sporting his trademark belt that has more gadgets and tools on it than Grammy's entire garage. I'm frozen in front of the bleachers when Mr. Simms finally notices me.

"Hey, Mr. Simms!" I call, waving.

He frowns before making his way over.

"Both gym classes are outside today," he says. "Back fields."

I shake my head. I was planning on fixing the bleachers myself, but this feels like the kind of opportunity I can't pass up. It's just about getting the wording right.

"I actually wanted to talk to you," I say. "During the last assembly I was in here and I noticed one of the railings was kind of loose. My bus came early that day, so I forgot to mention it. But they were talking about assembly in class just now and I remembered. I wanted to tell you about it so no one got hurt or anything."

His eyes land on the duct tape. He laughs. "Were you coming to fix it?"

I can't help grinning. "This was my backup plan."

"Smart thinking," Mr. Simms says. "Well, we don't want any accidents. Where was it?"

I pretend to scan the rows. "I was standing up near the top."

Mr. Simms leads the way. He runs a hand up the railing the whole time, testing each separate piece with a little push. "I think it's up there," I say, pointing. "The second from the top."

He skips a couple and sets his hand on the one from my vision. The railing responsible for Jeffrey Johnson's second death. "Doesn't look too bad. . . ." But as he gives it a good shove, the whole thing unhinges. Mr. Simms steadies himself and just barely manages to keep the whole railing from toppling over the side. "Good heavens! Looks like a few of the bolts popped out."

He doesn't even have to look as he reaches down into one of the pouches on his belt. He takes out a tool and a few shiny, new bolts. A second later he's down on one knee and lining up the frame of the railing. "So you can fix it?" I ask. "Just like that?"

"Just like that," Mr. Simms replies. "I'm glad you remembered. I'll have it good as new in a couple of minutes. What's your name again?"

"Celia Cleary."

He glances back and nods. "You can get back to class, but I'll put your name in for the Patriot Awards. No telling what could have happened if you hadn't said something."

The idea of getting any attention for this is already making me blush. I can imagine my mom finding out about the weekly honor and thinking it's the greatest thing in the world. I can also see Grammy standing in the background, making some sarcastic remark about being in the right place at the right time.

"No need for that!" I say. "It was nothing. I almost forgot!"

Mr. Simms starts tightening the first bolt. "But you didn't forget. Probably saved me a lot of trouble. Administration was asking me to nominate someone anyways! So thanks."

I'm standing there trying to figure out some way to convince him I'm not a hero when he looks back at me. "You better get back to class. Do you need a hall pass or something?"

I wave Mrs. Honea's clipboard. "Got one."

He turns his attention back to the railing, and I realize I've lost this battle. I walk back to Mrs. Honea's classroom. A part of me is dreading the attention I might get, but there's another part of me that's secretly nodding in approval. The railing *is* fixed, after all. Jeffrey Johnson's going to stumble later this afternoon, but now the railing will hold.

He won't fall, because of *me*.

Which means I saved him again.

CHAPTER NINE

The Assembly

Assemblies were designed in the Middle Ages as a form of torture. At least, I think I read that somewhere. I sit in the stands with the rest of our school and it *feels* like an actual fact.

I told a little white lie to Mom about there being a guest speaker. Today's assembly is focused—as usual— on the football team. Our cheerleading squad is out on the court now, trying out their newest routine before tonight's big game. I'm squeezed between Sophie and DeSean on the top row. Down on the court, Avery's being launched into the air by three other cheerleaders.

Sophie leans over. "Is it bad that I want her to slip?"

DeSean nods. "That is actually pretty bad, yeah."

Avery balances in the air, white shoes held tightly in the hands of the girls below her. She holds up a sign with the word *GO* painted in bright letters. When she raises the sign, the entire gymnasium cheers the word with her. It's all kind of annoying, but not so annoying that I'd actually want her to get hurt. Sophie's just a little more intense than I am.

"No broken bones," she clarifies. "Just an embarrassing stumble or something."

DeSean rolls his eyes. Listening to them, I feel a little weight in my chest. Both of them know that Avery and I got into an argument. They both know Avery stopped talking to me—and then stopped hanging out with us. But I didn't include the fact that Grammy's magic was at the center of it. I've never told them that I'd also be magical. There's a small part of me now that's afraid they'll react the way Avery did. Like I'm some kind of weirdo who they don't want to be around.

None of us would ever admit it, but Avery was the leader

of our group. She always came up with these funny hypothetical questions. She laughed the loudest and talked the most. Our group survived just fine, but we all miss her a little. Or I guess a lot.

The cheerleaders finish their routine before trotting back to their seats on the front row. I watch Avery and try to ignore the strange feeling in my chest as Principal Locklear walks out to center court. I get hit by a wave of déjà vu. I've seen this before. He walks past the Patriot mascot painted on the floor, taps the microphone once, and starts his announcements.

". . . all right. Don't forget to come out to all the games this week and really show that Patriot Pride! We're going to dismiss buses four, seven, nine, twelve, and eighteen."

I don't have to search the crowd. Jeffrey's a few rows below us, exactly where he sat in the vision. He stands up, and a few of the goofy soccer players sitting with him stand too. My stomach turns as they start pushing and shoving and laughing. I *know* that the problem is fixed, but I can still see the fatal accident playing on repeat in my head. Jeffrey adjusts his bag to squeeze by the girl at the end of the row, and the moment comes like a strike of secondhand lightning.

Hands shove out.

Jeffrey loses his balance.

But this time the bars hold.

He throws a look at one of the soccer players behind him. The two of them laugh it off. He's *alive*. He survived. Jeffrey repositions his bag again, and I can't help smiling as both feet touch safely down on the basketball court.

I watch him round the corner, and it might just be the best feeling in the world.

Locklear launches into a few other announcements. I sit there between DeSean and Sophie, who've restarted a conversation from lunch about zombies. I'm feeling so satisfied about another successful rescue that I almost don't notice DeSean tapping my shoulder.

"Cleary? Didn't your bus get called?"

I frown. Of course. I was so focused on saving Jeffrey that I didn't realize I'm on the same bus that he is. I scan the crowd and see Avery's gone. All the neighborhood kids are.

"Gotta run! See you guys!"

I make my awkward way down the row. Our bus got dismissed a while ago, so I'm two-stepping it down the bleachers. A teacher I don't recognize tells me to be careful, but I'm already booking it toward the exit. It's been a *long* day. The failed quiz. The successful rescue. Thinking about Avery. I don't want to add missing the bus to the list.

I'm halfway down the hall when an unexpected scent floods the room: campfire.

"No . . ."

I barely get the word out when my vision goes blank. The hallway vanishes, and I'm standing in the middle of the woods. I spy a few trails heading in different directions. Then Jeffrey is there. He's following a few of his soccer buddies. I get that first glimpse of them and then . . .

. . . the vision disappears.

There's a very firm and very real hand on my shoulder.

"Celia? Are you all right?"

I'm on the floor. DeSean is kneeling down beside me. My vision of the real world is still spinning a little. Even though I'm sitting in the hallway of my school again, I can still hear the boys talking as they walk and the sound of birds in the trees. I have to blink a few times to pull myself back to the present. DeSean has one of my notebooks from class tucked under one arm.

"I'm fine," I say. "Must have slipped."

He raises an eyebrow. "You left your math notes. I was trying to catch you before you got outside. From down the hallway it looked like you just kind of slumped. You sure you're all right? Maybe you have a concussion or something."

Or it could be the fact that I had a prophetic vision?

Definitely can't tell him that.

"I'm really fine. And I don't want to miss my bus."

He offers a hand to help me up. "I'll walk you out."

In some distant corner of my brain, I hear a cry for help. A branch is snapping? And then there's something that sounds like a splash. DeSean pulled my attention away from the vision. I can't see what's happening, but I'm still hearing it somehow. My mind races. When will Jeffrey and his friends walk through the woods? Tomorrow? A week from now? It takes a few seconds to realize DeSean's asking a question.

"You sure you're all right, Cleary?"

I nod. "I'm fine."

"I just tried to hand you your notebook." He waves it at me. "You kept on marching like a zombie."

"I feel like a zombie," I reply. "Didn't get enough sleep. That's all."

I take the notebook and stuff it into my book bag. I was so distracted that I didn't notice that most of the zippers are open. Clearly, I'm not at my best today. We turn the corner into the main atrium. The bus circle is looking pretty empty. Just a few buses chugging at a standstill as students file aboard. How long was I on the ground?

"You're number nine, right?" he asks. "Looks like it already took off."

I let out a huge sigh. "Great."

"No worries. My sister's picking me up today. Want to ride home with us?"

"Really? You don't mind?"

He shrugs. "You're not too far out of the way. Come on."

We have to weave through the crowd of stragglers. There

are a handful of parents gliding around the traffic circle like hawks. DeSean has us heading for the very front of the circle. There's a red car waiting in the no-parking zone. The windows are down and the music is pumping.

DeSean glances back before opening the door. "Let me do the negotiating."

I raise an eyebrow. "Negotiating? Negotiating what?"

He opens the door and leads the way into the back seat. The car smells brand-new. The floors are spotless. There's even a charger cord trailing back from the main console. DeSean snatches it as he slides across and plugs his phone in. I'm so distracted by the upgraded interior that it takes me a second to realize I've seen this car—and this driver—before.

She's wearing the same dark green makeup she was the other day. I can see her smirking at me in the rearview mirror.

"I charge extra for people who haven't figured out how to cross the road."

CHAPTER TEN

JoyRide™

I'm Tatyana."

She offers her hand, and about a thousand different bracelets bounce against one another.

"Celia Cleary."

Tatyana nods. "Glad to see you're still alive. I was worried you wouldn't make it this long."

"Do you two know each other?" DeSean asks, clearly confused.

"Almost introduced her to my front bumper last week," Tatyana replies. "Girl crossed the street without even looking. Good thing I've got better reactions than Cruz Ramirez."

DeSean rolls his eyes. "Her house is in the Green, Tatyana."

As I watch, Tatyana does about twenty things all at the same time. She briefly checks her makeup in the mirror. She shifts gears and glides around a soccer mom's van. One hand punches my address into her phone without looking. The other starts some kind of futuristic-looking timer that's attached to her car's dashboard. DeSean notices the last item and lets out a groan.

"Come on, Tatyana," he says. "This isn't a JoyRide."

She flashes a smile before merging perfectly into traffic. "Don't get your pants twisted. I'm tracking all my rides. I can get a tax write-off on all of it. Business 101. You're such a rookie."

"Rookie?" DeSean laughs. "Pretty sure the Sandwhich Stop outearned you last year."

Tatyana swerves down a back road I've never even noticed before. "Maybe on gross income? But my other investments doubled last year. Try and keep up, little bro."

DeSean looks annoyed by that, but his response is cut off as Tatyana swerves around another corner. I'm scanning the unfamiliar streets, trying to figure out where the heck we're going.

"Sorry . . . but what's a JoyRide?"

Tatyana reaches up and taps a massive sticker in the top-left corner of her windshield. I hadn't noticed it before. It's backward for us, but I can still make out the word *JoyRide* in fancy letters. It looks like a logo. "My company," Tatyana explains. "The only ridesharing experience designed exclusively for teenagers in the state of North Carolina."

DeSean glances over and sees my confusion. "It's a taxi service."

"More like an *experience*," Tatyana corrects. "I've been in operation for about three months now. I've got a ninety-nine percent approval rating and the best playlist in the industry. Here's my card."

She takes another sharp turn while simultaneously handing me a glitter-black business card with lipstick-red letters. I take it, still confused, and glance over at DeSean. He shakes his head.

"First ride is free," she says. "My rates are competitive. There are only a few Uber and Lyft drivers in our town, and most of them won't take someone under eighteen. My hours of operation are on the back. Just give me a shout if you ever need a ride."

I can't help pointing out the obvious. "My mom usually takes me places."

We take another turn, and I realize we're near the Green. I have no idea how we actually got here, though. "Told you, Tatyana," DeSean says. "Your target market is basically inexistent."

Tatyana's eyes find me in the rearview. "You'd be surprised how many people don't have a dependable ride. Besides, let's say you need to get Mom a present, but want to keep it on the down low? Call JoyRide. If you ever want to get home safe from a party that maybe Mom doesn't know about? Call JoyRide. If you ever *miss* your bus and Mom's too busy at work to pick you up right away? Call JoyRide. Full satisfaction guaranteed!"

She slides to a stop right where the bus usually drops me off.

DeSean nods at me. "Catch you on Monday, Celia."

I thank Tatyana for the ride before jumping out of the car. The door's barely closed before she jets forward and takes the first right. I frown a little, because I've always thought that way was a dead end. As I walk home, I pull out the card she gave me and run a finger over the bright letters. I'm almost to the front door before I realize what I'm holding.

This is a golden ticket.

I've been lucky so far. Jeffrey's first death was in walking distance. His second one just happened to be at school. But what if my next vision happens somewhere I can't walk to? Grammy doesn't really drive too much these days. Mom would totally catch on if I made too many random requests. So I tuck Tatyana's card into my back pocket and smile.

For the first time, it feels like I have an ace up my sleeve.

CHAPTER ELEVEN

Sort of Stalking

The ace up my other sleeve is the Cleary Family Guide Book.

When I get home, I go straight for it. DeSean interrupted me in the hallway. Which means I've got just half of the vision in my possession. I saw Jeffrey's second death multiple times. Dreamed about it whenever I fell asleep. I'm not sure if I have that kind of time. What if he's going hiking with his friends *today*?

On page 73, I find the passage I need: *Drinking cherry blossom tea can enhance a seer's ability.* There's a footnote that leads to an index. A few minutes later, I'm at the stove, mixing ingredients like a proper master of potions. The only thing missing is an old-school cauldron.

I'm stirring the tea when I realize Grammy isn't home. I frown, glancing across the empty living room, until I spot a note on the refrigerator in her handwriting.

Went swimming. Be back around 4.

Swimming? That's new. At least it gives me time to attempt the spell with no one else poking around and asking what I'm up to. I carefully remove the pot, turn off the heat, and pour a decent measure into my favorite mug. The directions aren't very helpful after that. The entry just says to "sip slowly so you don't burn your mouth," which feels more like hot-tea advice than magical advice. As I sip, my tongue curls up. It's a pleasant but dry taste.

Next step: summon the vision. The book has advice for that, too. I'm supposed to focus on one particular image from what I was shown of the future. I need to sit in a comfortable space. Close my eyes. And once I have that fixed in my mind, I'm supposed to physically lean forward.

I plunk down on the couch. It *is* comfortable. No doubt about that. I've spent an embarrassing number of hours on this couch binge-watching every show in existence. I close my eyes and try to remember what happened in the vision. There were trees everywhere. Jeffrey was walking behind his friends. He was wearing a backpack. It was sky blue. I focus on that. The white ties hanging from the zippers. The logo at the center that looked like a mountain sunrise.

Then I lean forward.

It's like falling asleep, instantly arriving in a dream. The living room is gone. I'm standing in the same forest I saw the other day, except now it's frozen in place. Jeffrey is caught midstride at the back of the group. The world colors in around him. It was hard to tell before. The vision came and went so quickly. Now I can count them and see who's with him. There are four boys walking through the woods.

The other three are all familiar faces. Hunter Jones is in one of my classes. Kind of a jerk. One time in elementary school he said I looked like an oversized chicken. Hard to forget a comment like that. Tyreek walks behind him. He's one of the class clowns. Always saying something funny. Never too serious. The fourth person is Everett. A lot of girls in the seventh grade have big crushes on him. He's got bleached-blond hair that runs almost to his shoulders. I don't really see the appeal. I think Jeffrey's a lot better-looking. . . .

My thoughts stutter to a halt.

Focus, Celia. You're here to save him.

I stand there for a second, waiting for the vision to begin. Nothing happens, though. Is this because it was interrupted the first time? Is this all I'll get to see?

Carefully I take a step closer. Everything snaps into motion. Voices fill the air. They're trudging down the trail. I have to hurry to keep up.

"That's *so* embarrassing, man," Hunter says. "What'd you do?"

Tyreek laughs. "Dude. I left. Didn't even go back upstairs to finish the movie."

They're navigating a trail. I'm half listening to their conversation and half eyeing the surrounding forest for clues. Where is this? Maybe somewhere near the greenway? It's kind of weird that I get to listen in to their conversations. Does this count as stalking? Sort of stalking?

"What did Shea do?"

Tyreek shrugs. "Don't know. We haven't talked since that night. There's no way to come back from that, man. I clogged up the toilet at my crush's house. Water was leaking *everywhere*. I'm just lucky she doesn't go to our school, bro. I'd have to drop out and have my mom homeschool me."

The others laugh. They've picked up their pace. Clearly heading somewhere.

"What about you, Jeffrey?" Hunter asks. "Can you beat that one?"

I see the way his face flushes with color. He nods to himself, like he's trying to gather his courage to speak. "I've got a good one. Back in fourth grade. I had a crush on Meg Quinn."

"She moved, right?" Everett asks.

Jeffrey nods, like that fact is a huge relief. "I really liked her, so I got my mom to take me to the mall before Valentine's Day. I picked her out some jewelry."

"Jewelry?" Tyreek is cracking up. "In fourth grade?"

As they're talking, Everett pulls out his phone. He's checking a message. I want to hear the rest of Jeffrey's story, but a light bulb goes off in my head. This is my chance to figure out the *when* of this vision. I dart forward, invisible to them, and glance over Everett's shoulder. The date winks back at me: March 12. Tomorrow. This death happens tomorrow.

Jeffrey is still telling his story.

". . . I just shoved it in her desk when no one was looking. It was in this brown paper bag. She found it a few minutes later. It actually worked. She really liked it a lot."

Hunter throws a scowl back at him. "How is that embarrassing?"

"Well, I forgot to put my name on it," Jeffrey answers. "She asked who it was from. There was no way I was going to answer in front of everyone. I hesitated. And that's when her eyes landed on Chris Showers. . . ."

"No way," Tyreek says. "No way."

"She asked if it was from him. And Chris said yes! I couldn't believe it. He took the credit for it. I had to watch them sip chocolate milk together all through fifth grade. I never told her."

Hunter and Tyreek are cackling. "We need to get Chris out here instead of you," Hunter says between laughs. "Dude is bold."

Everett just shakes his head. I can tell it was hard for Jeffrey to share that story. It's like he wants it to be funny, but there's still some sting to the memory. Even though it *is* embarrassing, it's also super cute. What kind of fourth grader thinks to buy someone jewelry? The look on his face has me wishing I could walk through the vision and give him a hug.

"Here it is."

Hunter's words sound ominous somehow. The woods clear. We're slightly elevated. Down below, there's a pond. Or a lake? I have to squint for a second to figure out what it really is. I've only ever seen pictures. The Rock Quarry. I know a few classmates who come here. Avery talked about it, back when we were still talking. It's more of a high-school spot. The old quarry filled with water years ago. Kids come here to jump off the trees and ledges, splashing into the deep cold water below. I've never been allowed to come because it's super dangerous. Every ten years or so, there's a bad accident. I'm pretty sure Mom even litigated one of the cases.

"Where's the best place to jump?" Tyreek asks.

There are other voices in the distance. A few people are floating in the water on noodles or rafts. I'm trying to get a better look when I hear it—we all do. A cry for help. Somewhere right below where we're standing, just out of sight. Someone needs help. There's another shout. All four of the boys freeze in place. Like deer in headlights.

Until Jeffrey launches into motion. While the others hesitate, he sprints around the corner, out of sight. Ready to save the person who needs help. The moment he vanishes—the vision vanishes too. My living room *pops* back into existence.

"He went to save them. . . ."

I don't have to see the rest of the vision to know that meant risking his own life in the process. Which most likely means that something bad happens down in the water. I have the facts now. I know where and I know when. But how do I keep them away from the quarry?

I'm sitting there, deep in thought, when I notice the TV was left on again. The main image for *Vampire High* is on the screen. It takes a second to remember what the last episode was about. My mind lands on an idea. I search on my phone for the right number. It rings.

"Hello. Parks Service. This is Jan."

"Hey Jan! I just wanted to report something."

I can hear someone rummaging around.

"Sure. Go ahead."

"Well, it's something that's going to happen. Tomorrow at four p.m. There's a big party planned at the Rock Quarry. It sounds like *everyone* is going to be there. And I'm pretty sure there's going to be alcohol involved." This is literally word for word from the last episode I watched. Mom *tsk*ed a few times when we watched the actual party scene. "I'm just worried about my friends. I don't want them to get in any trouble. . . ."

Jan makes a noise. "Hmm. Okay. And what was your name again?"

I hang up the phone. I know the Parks Department isn't very big in our town, but there's no way they'll ignore a direct tip like that. They'll send a park ranger over there to tell kids the quarry isn't open. No one will go in the water, which means no one will struggle in the water, which means Jeffrey won't have anyone to save. I raise my tea in a celebratory cheer to no one. I might never get tired of rescuing if I could do it from the couch.

"Pretty sure saving lives deserves a reward."

I nestle under the blanket. A few minutes later, I'm fast asleep.

CHAPTER TWELVE

The Problem(s) with Prophecies

It works like a charm.

The next afternoon, I keep an eye on Jeffrey after school. His friends take the bus home with him, but they never head out for the quarry. Instead, they stay in the backyard playing Spikeball. Someone must have spread the word that the quarry was shut down for the day. All because of my phone call.

I savor the taste of another victory until about 8:12 a.m. the next day. Winning at prophecies means I'm starting to lose at other things. In first period, we get our most recent science test back. My eyes trail down the page, and my heart sinks straight to the floor. It's my very first D on a big exam. The news doesn't get any better as I go through the day. I earned a C– on my social studies test and made a huge mistake on my math quiz too. As I think through my other classes, I realize I might have bad grades in every single class except for art.

Mrs. Honea even pulls me aside to inform me I'll be spending half of my lunch in study hall for the rest of the week. Great. I walk into the hallway, still kind of dazed, and run right into Sophie. She's always blunt, but this time her words really catch me off guard.

"Hey. Are you pulling an Avery on us?"

I stare back at her. "What? Pulling an Avery?"

"Vanishing. Like she did. Abandoning us."

"Of course not, Sophie! What are you talking about?"

"You've missed three lunches in a row," she explains. "And you were supposed to come over yesterday to make T-shirts with me. I texted you and everything. What happened?"

It's not hard to figure out. I was trying to keep an eye on Jeffrey's activities. Making sure I saved his life, and I forgot all about her in the process. "I'm sorry, Sophie. I've been distracted. My grades aren't good. It's hard to explain. I'm not pulling an Avery. I wouldn't do that."

I want to promise her that all this will be over soon, but I realize I *can't* promise that. Unless I find an answer in our family's magical guide, a loophole or something, this isn't a temporary situation. I could be saving Jeffrey Johnson for the rest of his life.

"Good," Sophie replies. "Because I'm tired of seeing your grandma more than I see my best friend. No offense to your grandma. She's really sweet."

"You're right. I—wait. What?"

"Your grandma swims at the same pool as me."

I frown. "You swim?"

Sophie barely resists rolling her eyes. "Every morning before school."

"But you're not on the swim team?"

"I don't like competition. That stuff stresses me out. I just like . . . the way the water feels. I've liked it since I was really little. It always calms me down."

I nod. Kind of like walks on the greenway work for me. I can't believe I never knew that Sophie liked to swim. I didn't realize how much Grammy likes it either. I knew she signed up for an afternoon class at the local aquatic center, but now she's going in the mornings too? Maybe it's a calming activity for seers or something. I'll have to ask her. The last time she was this into a hobby, she accidentally cross-stitched a family friend's engagement announcement into a blanket and spoiled the whole surprise.

My thoughts are so distracting that it takes me a second to process the other part of what Sophie just said. She called me her *best friend*. I realize that's true. She and DeSean are my best friends, now that Avery's gone. But I know I haven't really been treating her like one. Best friends don't just vanish without an explanation.

"I'm sorry, Sophie. I'll make it up to you."

That earns another nod. "It's fine. Want to walk to second period?"

"Only if you tell me which swim stroke is your favorite."

Sophie groans as we start walking. "Don't be weird, Cleary."

I smile at her. It feels like I've temporarily patched up one problem, but the other one is burning a hole in my back pocket. Those grades won't cut it in the Cleary residence. I decide that I can't tell Mom about them. Not yet. Not until I've had time to pull them back up.

Time is funny, though.

It's like the more you pay attention to it, the faster it slips through your fingers. That week, I save Jeffrey two more times. My ability to control the vision is improving. I have the cherry blossom tea to thank for that. I learn how to navigate around the future glimpses, pausing and unpausing at will. Grammy called me a "Precognition Engineer," and I'm kind of thinking she could be right. *Precognition* just means I see a glimpse of the future. The *Engineer* part comes from the fact that I can examine each detail like I'm the director on a movie set.

Saving Jeffrey *feels* like progress, but Grammy preaches caution every time I bring him up. She's not trying to stop me from helping him, but at every turn, she reminds me there's no way to alter his fate. I am very grateful, though, when she starts offering other magical advice.

"Cherry blossom tea, huh? Try adding a spoonful of honey next time."

The pinch of honey alleviates my headaches. I learn that repeating a key phrase before entering a vision keeps me from collapsing like I did in the hallway at school. The Cleary Family Guide Book offers a thousand little tricks, but none of the pages I come across have the answer that I really need.

I hunt through paragraphs and footnotes. On long walks with Grammy, I ask questions that might offer clues to help me. Every night when Mom and I sit there watching *Vampire High*, my mind traces back through all the details, trying to figure out a way to distract death from Jeffrey Johnson once and for all. I need to find the answer soon.

Any hope of a normal life depends on it.

CHAPTER THIRTEEN

The Crab Shack

I'm staring out the bus window on the way home from school.

The new center of my universe—Jeffrey Johnson—sits somewhere in the back section of the bus. After our first conversation, he hasn't really visited my area of the bus. I was annoyed by that, but then I remembered I was the one who abandoned *him* the first time we talked. Maybe he's still offended?

As the wheels of the bus rumble and the trees blur, I actually find a moment of quiet. No thoughts about Jeffrey or my bad grades or Avery or whatever. I just look out the window without a care in the world. Naturally, that's when the next vision comes.

The bus window vanishes.

Jeffrey Johnson's standing in front of me with his soccer bag over one shoulder. He always appears first. It's like my mind recognizes him, the same way you might recognize a familiar scent. The rest of the vision colors in around him. He's standing on a sidewalk facing a busy road. Behind him, there's a narrow strip of grass, then a half-filled parking lot. It's bright out. Sunlight reflects off windshields and scorches the blacktop. Jeffrey is looking down at his phone. In the distance, there's a glowing red sign: THE CRAB SHACK.

I breathe a sigh of relief. Some of the locations have been super vague. Random places that forced me to research for hours online. I know the Crab Shack, though. We went there for my seventh birthday. A day that was only memorable because one of my cousins attempted a rescue mission to smuggle lobsters out of their display tank.

I pause the vision and walk forward. Thankfully, his

phone is already out. That makes my job a lot easier. I glance over one shoulder, and my eyes land instinctively on the timestamp: March 24, 1:00 p.m. Before I can move away, though, another detail catches my eye. The picture on the background of his phone has changed. I've been looking at his phone a *lot* lately. Usually it features random soccer players doing random sportsball moves.

Not this one.

It literally looks like a picture from one of those Awkward Family Photo collections. Jeffrey's wearing an absurd-looking sweater that has to be from his dad's wardrobe. It's a little too big on him at the sleeves, and the pattern looks straight out of 2003. He's deadpanning at the camera, and his hands are set on the shoulders of someone about half his size.

"So that's your little brother. . . ."

My words echo. It takes me a second to remember I'm *in* a vision. He can't actually talk to me, and it doesn't matter because the kid's face confirms it. He looks just like Jeffrey. His hair is even styled the same way. I'd guess he's about five years old.

I look closer at the picture and can't help smiling. He's wearing one of their dad's sweaters too. It's so big on him that the only thing I can see underneath are his little sneakers. He's matching Jeffrey's serious face, but you can tell that they're both on the verge of busting out laughing.

And it hits me like a lightning strike.

"You have a brother."

And a dad. And a mom. A whole family. I stumble back as the answer to why I've been trying *so* hard all this time hits me right in the forehead. Jeffrey's not some random person. Not to them. He's a big brother and a first son and a best friend. To most of us, he's the quiet kid who lives on the corner, but not to them. It feels like I just got the breath knocked out of my lungs.

"I'm going to save you," I whisper. "I promise, I'm going to save you."

Before the vision can begin, though, I'm dragged back to the present by a voice. It's a little like déjà vu because I blink a few times and find myself staring at Jeffrey Johnson. He's got different clothes on, though. No sign of the Crab Shack. We're back on the bus.

He's smiling at me with an eyebrow raised.

"Wow," he says. "You must have been having a cool dream."

"Yeah. Huh. What?"

"You were doing this weird arm movement with your eyes closed," he says. "Like you were reaching out to someone. Or flying, maybe? Can you fly in your dreams? I always dream that I'm . . . fixing a go-kart with Mr. Ferris or something. Super random."

"Hey!" our bus driver calls from the front. "This isn't an Uber. We've got other stops."

Jeffrey smiles at me, but starts trudging obediently to the front. I grab my own bag, wiping an embarrassing amount of drool from one corner of my mouth, and follow. The realizations are still hammering in my chest. I can almost picture little threads attaching Jeffrey to his mom, and his dad, and his brother. All the bright little moments they've shared that no one knows about but them.

In my imagination, death's standing off in the shadows, ready to snip them, one by one.

CHAPTER FOURTEEN

Grounded

It's a pleasant surprise to find Mom waiting at home.

She never gets off early. I take two steps into the kitchen, though, and the word *pleasant* evaporates. It's still a surprise, but everything about Mom's posture tells me this will not be a pleasant conversation. My eyes trail to the kitchen table. There's an opened envelope and a single piece of paper. It looks alarmingly like a report card.

Mom tilts her head. "Sit."

I know Mom doesn't have any magic, not like me and Grammy, but the tone of her voice might as well be a spell.

My body obeys like I'm being pulled across the room on puppet-like strings. I shrink into a chair that's strategically across the table from her. Usually the angrier she gets, the higher the chance spit will be involved. I'd like to steer clear of the blast radius.

"Would you like an opportunity to explain?"

I squint at the report card, then at her, thinking. Mom's a master at ripping apart opening arguments. Better to keep things as simple as possible. "I've been a little distracted."

"A little?" she echoes. "Define a little."

I sigh. "I can pull them up."

"You *will* pull them up. Celia, you're almost failing a class. That's not like you at all. I need to know . . ." She trails off, and I can tell she's entering uncomfortable territory. "Is this connected to magic at all? I haven't asked much about it—I know—but I just . . . Is it that?"

I shake my head quickly and reach for the first obvious excuse.

"Avery abandoned our friend group."

It feels *so* wrong. It's a lie. And I know it's a lie. But Mom absolutely buys it. I can see her face shift from anger to sympathy. She bites her lip, a little unsure how to proceed.

"I noticed she doesn't come over anymore. I thought it was just . . . a little fight."

I dip my chin and nod. My guilt doubles. Lying feels a lot like digging a hole in the ground and hoping I don't accidentally fall in at some point later. I try to end the conversation as quickly as possible.

"I'll do better. It's starting to feel more normal. I promise."

For about two seconds, I think I actually got away with it. Mom is nodding carefully, watching me with more understanding. "That explains the grades. Not the lie."

I glance up. How does she *know* I'm lying? It's like some kind of mom radar went off.

"But I didn't . . ."

"Celia Eleanor Cleary." I fall silent. The combination of her lawyer voice and my middle name is like a superweapon. "Mrs. Honea's note says that these reports went home with students last week. You were supposed to have me sign it and turn it back in. It even says that having it signed would have replaced one of your zeroes. But you didn't bring yours home. You didn't show it to me. She had to send it to me herself."

Busted. I know the original report card is jammed into the front section of my book bag. And I know I didn't give it to Mom for this exact reason. She's waiting for an answer, and I can tell there's no way to squirm my way out of this one. "I didn't want you to be mad."

"I am mad," she said. "I get a few bad grades. I get that life happens. But you've never lied to me before, Celia. Not about something like this."

I nod again and know better than to make direct eye contact.

"You're grounded. I think our plans for the twenty-fourth have to change."

Alarm bells are going off. That date has been stamped into the front of my brain. I can see that number staring up at me from the brightly lit surface of Jeffrey's phone. That's the next day that he's scheduled to die. I frown at Mom. How could she know . . .

"Our plans?"

"No Pimiento Cheese Festival over in the Village."

It takes effort not to breathe out a sigh of relief. I'd forgotten all about the festival. I definitely hadn't pieced together that it was the same day as Jeffrey's death. It's actually kind of perfect that we're not going to go. What are the odds I could have saved him *and* not awkwardly bailed on Mom?

"Okay. I understand."

"Instead, you'll be in your room all day. Mrs. Honea is collecting a packet of worksheets from your other teachers. She said you can make up some of the work. That's stage one of being grounded."

"But Mom . . ."

"Hey. This is a pretty light sentence, Celia. You promised to do better. This is how it starts. You'll sit in your room this Saturday and you'll do your work. No questions asked."

I grind my teeth in frustration, because no matter how hard I think about it, there's no explanation that will work. I don't feel like I can tell my mom how much of my time has gone toward saving Jeffrey Johnson. Sure, she knows I have magic, but I doubt she'd approve of just how much of my schedule centers around him—instead of homework and school and everything else. Not to mention she might make me stop if she knew that some of the rescues weren't exactly putting me in the safest situations. Which means I also can't tell her that being stuck inside on Saturday is a life-or-death situation for Jeffrey.

Instead, I'm forced to nod in agreement. "Yes, ma'am."

Mom sweeps in and kisses my forehead. "I'm sorry about the Avery thing. We can talk about it if you want. Grammy will be home from swim class soon. Let's get dinner ready."

She starts pulling ingredients out of the fridge. As I set my book bag down, I notice a little slash of red. In the front pocket, there's a familiar and flashy business card. I'd almost forgotten that I put it there, but it's the card Tatyana gave me the day she drove me home. I tuck it into a back pocket before heading over to help chop vegetables.

I'm about halfway through cutting an onion when all the pieces fall into place. I know what I'm going to do. A smile stretches over my face.

It's the perfect plan.

CHAPTER FIFTEEN

"Real" Homework

I'm up early Saturday morning.

Someone's downstairs making the first round of coffee. Normally I'd head down and hang out, but step one in my plan is to finish *all* my homework. Mrs. Honea handed off the packet of work on Friday, and it's annoyingly large. My book bag looks like an overgrown turtle. I had to bring home every single one of my textbooks to cover all the work that I missed.

History breezes by first. It's mostly a game of search and destroy. I work my way through the entire Cold War in about an hour. Language arts is next. We're studying Langston Hughes poems. I've annotated all three of them—highlighting metaphors with one pen and marking the allusions with another—when Mom makes her first appearance.

Right on schedule.

"Celia?" She looks surprised to find me at my desk. "Look at you. Already working?"

I point to my completed stack. "The Renaissance didn't stand a chance."

She smiles. "Conquering Europe. That calls for bacon and eggs. I'll bring some up."

I turn back to my worksheet as she slips out of the room. A big breakfast is a part of Mom's weekend rhythm. I'm counting on her to go through the same routine she always goes through. My plan kind of depends on it. I'm halfway through my science worksheet on single-celled organisms when Mom bustles back in with a plate of food. "How's it going, honey?"

I snatch a piece of bacon. "Better now."

She eyes the papers in front of me. "Amoebas, huh?"

"The guy who discovered them has like eight names."

She smiles. "I'm proud of you for taking the initiative this morning."

I want to beam with pride. Books are piled all over my desk. I've already finished about half of the homework, but it's kind of ridiculous that I got this far behind. Even if I had good reason to.

"I'm sorry, Mom."

"Me too. It sounds like we both got a little distracted." She kisses my head. "I should have noticed something was up way before now. I'm here if you need to talk, all right? No matter how busy I might look."

I nod to her. "Thanks."

She slips out of the room again, and I start racing through the rest of the work. I make sure to complete everything carefully, though, because the only thing worse than doing all this would be having to do it *again*. I occasionally glance up at the clock just to make sure I don't lose track of time.

Jeffrey's cell phone in the vision said 1:00 p.m. I tried to build in at least an hour's worth of wiggle room just in case something goes wrong. The next step of the plan depends on Mom.

At exactly 11:33, there's another knock. She peeks her head in, and I almost jump out of my chair in celebration. She's wearing her slightly tighter-fitting workout clothes. She's got a water bottle in one hand and a key fob in the other. "I'm going to go to the gym, sweetie."

"Sounds good. Hey! I'm on my last worksheet. If I finish, can I duck outside for a little?"

She crosses the room to make an inspection. I was careful to leave the folder of conquered homework out on display. The textbooks I'm finished with are stacked up like evidence too.

"You're still grounded," she reminds me. "If Grammy wants to go on a walk, that's fine. Otherwise, rules are rules."

At the exact moment she closes the door, I dart toward my phone. Most of my friends lose cell privileges when they're grounded. Mom never asks for mine because I really don't spend that much time on it. I hold my phone's camera up to Tatyana's business card. It takes a second to focus and scan the number, and the call immediately goes through.

I tiptoe back across the room, listening for noises in the hallway. Mom's heading down the stairs. The footsteps are slowly fading when a voice jumps to life on the other end of the phone.

"JoyRide services. Tatyana speaking."

"Uhh ... Tatyana ... This is Celia Cleary."

"DeSean's friend," she says without hesitation. "What's up?"

"Are you available? For driving?"

"I'm dropping someone off right now. You're over in the Green?"

I can feel the garage rumbling open beneath my feet. "301 Town Home."

There's a brief hesitation. "I can be there in ten."

"Perfect," I reply. "Oh. And can you pick me up near the park? Not outside the house?"

I can hear the grin in Tatyana's voice as she says, "Off the radar. No problem."

She hangs up. I move the final worksheet into the completed folder. The gym is about fifteen minutes away. Mom will be there for an hour and a half. It'll take her another fifteen minutes to get home. It should give me just enough time to save Jeffrey Johnson.

All without getting grounded again.

CHAPTER SIXTEEN

In the Details

Downstairs is ominously empty.

I was ready for an encounter with Grammy. I kind of thought she'd be waiting at the foot of the stairs to talk me out of lying to Mom *again*. She has an intuition about stuff like that. Ever since I was little, she'd randomly appear at just the right moment to stop me from doing something really foolish. Not this time. A glance through the kitchen window shows she's out back, working in her garden. Everything I learned in kindergarten is a reminder that I should tell *someone* where I'm going, but Grammy's too much of a wild card. The last thing I need at this point is a complication.

It's easier to just save Jeffrey and get home before anyone finds out.

I slip out the front door, lock it behind me, and head up the street. There's parking on each side of the Green—which is the open area from which our little section of the neighborhood gets its name. No sign of Tatyana's red car yet. It's hot enough that I head for the shaded corner that's closest to the road. I check my phone one more time, but there aren't any missed calls. I wander impatiently through the cover of trees, turn a corner, and almost run smack into Avery.

She's alone. That's new. Usually Jordan Lyles is somewhere nearby. My stomach sinks a little as I remember that this is where the two of us used to go after school. We would drag our hammocks up to this grove and hang out for hours. My stomach sinks even more when I remember this is also where our fight happened.

I'm about to apologize for intruding when I realize that she's crying.

"Avery?"

She whips around. "What?"

There's so much anger in her voice that I take a step back. For the thousandth time, I just feel like running away. She's made it clear enough that she doesn't want me around. It takes effort to move toward her instead. I keep my voice soft. "Avery. Are you okay?"

She turns away from me. "I'm fine."

I want to leave. There's a small voice in my head that reminds me that she's the one who abandoned me. Why should I try to do something nice for her? Instead, I reach out and set a hand on her shoulder. I'm kind of amazed when she doesn't pull away.

"Do you want to talk about it?"

She makes an annoyed noise, but I can tell that just like the anger in her voice, the annoyance isn't actually meant for me. "Jordan broke up with me."

In the distance, I see a red car make the turn into our neighborhood. There's a little burst of life from the engine as it heads in our direction. Tatyana is here.

"Never liked him anyways," I whisper.

That actually drags a laugh out of Avery. It's amazing, though, how quickly it transforms into a sob. "But I did." She wipes her eyes and glances at me. "Don't have any spells for that, do you?"

And with that, she walks away. It feels like a cheap shot. It's not my fault that Jordan broke up with her. And Grammy isn't the reason her parents split up either. I try to remind myself that she's hurting and that it's not my fault, but that doesn't take the sting out of her words.

A sharp *beep* cuts through my thoughts. Tatyana is leaning across the front seat of her car. "Time is money, Cleary!"

I jog over. My mind is still being pulled in twenty different directions. I'm mad that Avery said what she said. I'm annoyed that I couldn't figure out the *right* thing to say. And I'm sad that we can't just be friends again. I don't have time for any of that, though, because I've got to save Jeffrey without getting in trouble with my mom. It's time to get moving.

I climb into the back seat, still a bundle of nerves, and Tatyana nods to me in the mirror.

"Where we heading?"

"The Crab Shack," I say. "It's over on Davie Drive."

But Tatyana's already entering in the address. She double-checks her mirrors and whips back through the neighborhood. "Usually people sneak out at night, you know? And if they're sneaking out, usually it's to somewhere a little more questionable than the Crab Shack."

I imagine the restaurant's glowing sign behind Jeffrey Johnson.

"I'm not sneaking out."

Tatyana lifts an eyebrow but doesn't ask any more questions. I glance at my phone. It's almost noon. We'll get there with plenty of time to spare. I've been going back through the vision in my head. Jeffrey's standing on the sidewalk that separates the parking lot from a busy road. It's the second car-crash scenario. There's a part of me that wishes I could just sit him down and tell him to not stand so *close* to the road. That should be like a basic rule of life for all people.

I can fix this one easily enough, though. I just have to get Jeffrey away from the curb. The first idea I had was to tip one of the waiters in the restaurant. Maybe delay Jeffrey's meal or something? If that doesn't work, I'm thinking I might be able to pull him into a conversation? I'd rather not interfere directly, but as long as it's not too obvious, Jeffrey won't be suspicious.

Tatyana has us swinging into the parking lot way quicker than I expected.

I start pulling out cash when I realize that my plan has one very distinct problem. I knew I needed Tatyana to drive me out here, but I totally forgot she's my only way home. Every club meeting and sleepover I've ever had ended with Mom or Grammy picking me up.

"Thanks," I say. "How much is it for you to wait?"

Tatyana shrugs. "How long will you be?"

"Maybe thirty minutes?"

"I can start the meter," she says. "I'll give you a slight discount since you know DeSean. But it works as if I'm still driving you around. It will track the time, because that's time I could be using to get other rides. Got it?"

It's nice of her to give me a discount, but I also realize I might be testing the limits of my birthday money.

"So how much?"

"Ride here. Wait time. Ride back." Tatyana runs the calculation. "Probably twenty bucks?"

"Okay. I'll try to make it quick."

Tatyana turns up her music as I exit the vehicle. The parking lot is half-empty. There's a swirl of families coming and going. I head for the entrance to the Crab Shack and can't help feeling there's something off. My seer senses feel unnerved. I'm not even sure if that's the right word, or if it's just intuition of some kind? Maybe it's the aura thing that Grammy mentioned?

The feeling has me focusing even more.

There's a family ahead of me, talking to the hostess. I use the distraction to move through the restaurant. I stick to the aisle that's nearest the kitchen. I pause near the bathrooms and look into the main dining areas. *Blue hoodie, blue hoodie, blue hoodie.* There's no sign of him. I decide to wait by the bathrooms for a few minutes just in case he's inside.

A few minutes pass. Nothing.

I move back through the room a second time. Maybe he took the hoodie off while eating? One of the waitresses gets annoyed by how slowly I'm walking, but she eventually bustles past. I'm careful to look at every single table. He's not here. I head back for the front and pause by the hostess station.

"Hey. Are there any other rooms? Or dining areas?"

She shakes her head. "This is it. Are you looking for someone?"

I nod distractedly. "Yeah. Maybe they're not here yet. Thanks."

After one more long look at the dining area, I head outside. This is so weird. I thought for sure that he'd be inside the restaurant. I walk back through the parking lot and try to draw on my memory of the vision again.

He was standing on the sidewalk, not in the actual parking lot. I know that the car that's going to crash comes from the road. And I remember that he looked like he was waiting for someone to pick him up. Moving in that direction, I find the exact location. It feels a little off for some reason. I glance both ways. There are a few other restaurants on my right. Maybe he's in one of those? I don't remember him *walking* in the vision, though. He was sweaty, like he'd just come from a game. I know he was holding his soccer bag. . . .

"What am I missing?"

There's a little honk. I realize I'm standing about thirty feet away from Tatyana.

"I thought you were eating," she calls. "What's up?"

I head back to the car and climb into the back seat. "I was looking for someone."

"Aha!" Tatyana makes a satisfied noise. "So it was a secret *rendezvous*. I love it."

"What? No. It's nothing like that."

"Right, right, right . . . ," she says. "So he didn't show?"

"Not yet," I say. "But it's not like that. Is it okay if I just wait here?"

"As long as you don't mind paying," she says, tapping the meter with one finger.

Which means we wait. My stomach starts doing back-flips as the clock ticks closer and closer to one p.m. I've never gotten to this point without a solution in place. That uncomfortable feeling is in the air again too. The hairs on the back of my neck are standing up.

Something is wrong.

Maybe I read the wrong date?

It'd be so annoying if I did all this—lied to my mom and everything—and didn't even need to save him. "Be right back."

I climb out of the car and walk back to the spot—or at least what I *think* is the spot. The angles are right. The Crab Shack stands in the distance. There's the sidewalk, the strip of grass, and then the parking lot fronting the building. Trees are on the right. In about fifteen minutes, Jeffrey Johnson is supposed to stand right here as a car comes peeling off the main road. I don't get it. Where the heck is he?

And then one tiny, almost unnoticeable detail catches my eye.

I take a step forward, squinting. "Oh no. No, no, no . . ."

The Crab Shack sign. The whole thing is backlit with red light, but for the first time, I notice that the *a* in the word

Shack has shorted out. That detail is wrong. In my vision, the whole sign was working just fine. And that can mean only one thing.

I sprint back to Tatyana's car. "Hey. Is there *another* Crab Shack?"

She frowns for a second, then nods. "Yeah. Off of 61. Over by Freshland."

"I need to get there *now*."

My brain enters full-scale panic mode. I slam on my seat belt as Tatyana directs us out into traffic. For the first time, I find myself wishing she'd go just a little faster. My phone blinks to life. Thankfully, there aren't any missed calls from Mom yet. We vault across town.

It's 12:47.

I'm running out of time.

Tatyana doesn't need any reminders that this is urgent. It's not like she's speeding or anything that would get us in trouble. She just slides through traffic like she's playing the world's easiest video game. Never once does she make the wrong turn, or get in the wrong lane. I find myself wishing time would freeze or slow down the way it does in the movies. Instead, it feels like someone has picked up my hourglass and is shaking it, stealing precious seconds from me. My eyes track Tatyana's progress on the phone, and I know we're still a minute away. Time is running *out*.

She makes one more turn, darts around another driver, and swings into the parking lot at exactly one o'clock. I almost slam my face into the window trying to get a look at Jeffrey.

He's there.

Standing right where he stood in the vision. His eyes are down on his phone as he waits by the curb. For a brief second, I can see death in the air around him. The dark threads are reaching down, nearly touching his shoulders. Tatyana darts into the spot right ahead of us. I slam the door open and almost clip the vehicle parked there. I don't bother closing the door. There's no time. Tatyana shouts something, but I don't catch the words. I'm already sprinting.

A sharp squeal of tires.

Jeffrey looks up. His eyes go wide.

I've never been very athletic, but I am *very* well informed.

I know exactly where the car is coming and how fast and at what angle. I've memorized this vision. I've done my homework.

And so I skid to a perfect stop behind him. My hands snatch for his soccer bag. Jeffrey's eyes are still locked on the spinning vehicle. But I give his bag a massive tug. He stumbles back toward me—and toward the safety of the parking lot.

"What the . . ."

He's a lot taller than me, but as he stumbles, I use the momentum and give him a huge shove away from the road. He hits the ground hard and I dive after him. Distantly I notice Tatyana crossing the parking lot and shouting something.

A second later one of the cars jumps the curb.

I have Jeffrey pinned beneath me as it slams into the sign about ten feet behind us. We keep our heads down as glass shatters and parts go flying. In any other moment, I'd be freaking out to be this close to a boy. But my chest heaves and I'm just happy he's alive. Jeffrey glances past me and sees the wreckage.

"Whoa! You saved me!"

CHAPTER SEVENTEEN

Safe and Sound

In the back of Tatyana's car, things are getting awkward. We glide across town to get back to our neighborhood. Jeffrey's sitting in the back seat with me, and he's been ranting for about ten minutes now. He was going to wait for the public bus, but Tatyana insisted he ride home with us after almost being in an accident. At this point, he's pretty much ready to put me in my own Marvel comic strip.

"It was like you appeared out of thin air," he says for the third time. "And you're really strong, too. I thought I was getting body-slammed by a professional wrestler or something."

My brain is chasing too many thoughts to attempt a response. I'm thinking about the fact that I have a missed call from Mom now. There's Tatyana, too. She keeps glancing at me in the rearview mirror with narrowed eyes. I can tell she thinks that there's something weird about what just happened. I'm hoping she'll chalk it up as a coincidence.

"I just froze," Jeffrey is saying. "You see people in movies and stuff, and you never think you'd be the person who just freezes. But when that car was coming for me, I couldn't move."

I nod distractedly.

"But *you* didn't freeze," he says. "It was so clutch. Your reaction skills were amazing."

Thankfully, he doesn't ask why I was right behind him or what I was doing at the Crab Shack. He doesn't realize how many times he was already supposed to die. I'm the only one who knows just how many times death has written the end of his story. He's breathing a sigh of relief that I don't ever get to breathe, because I know another vision is coming.

It doesn't end here. It won't stop today.

Jeffrey is still singing my praises as Tatyana pulls into a parking spot near the Green. He shoves out on his side, and I almost shout at him because it's on the road-facing side and he barely even looked. Instead, I use the distraction to hand over about half of my birthday money to Tatyana.

"Thanks for the ride."

She locks eyes with me. "That was . . . weird . . . but . . . at least he's cute?"

I take a deep breath. Tatyana is smart. I can tell she's trying to piece together exactly what happened. I might need her services in the future, though, so I'm kind of hoping she'll just overlook the strangeness and take the money. I nod my thanks, leave an extra ten dollars from my birthday supply, and duck out of the car.

Jeffrey's there. I'm not sure why I thought he was going to leave? As I close the door, he falls into step like we always walk home together. "So what are you up to today?" he asks.

His question surprises me. Is he trying to hang out or something?

"Uhh . . ."

Everything about this feels *awkward*. It's not just the crazy day or the overwhelming thoughts. It's walking alone with a boy for the first time and talking about *hanging out*. I glance over. It's a huge relief that Jeffrey looks as awkward as I feel.

"I mean, we don't have to," he says quickly. "I was just asking."

It takes me a second to remember part two of my plan.

"... Oh yeah! I'm grounded!"

I shout the words and start running down the street. Mom will be home any minute now. I have an image of her standing in the kitchen with that same you-know-what-you-did look on her face from the day before. Jeffrey shouts something from behind me, but I know he's safe for now, and that's all that matters.

Mom's car isn't back in the driveway. She could turn the corner any second. I'm surprised to see the garage door open. Did I leave it that way? Grammy's silver Accord sits in the same spot as always. I slip through the garage and shoulder into the kitchen.

I almost jump in fright. It isn't Mom. It's Grammy.

She's standing by the refrigerator in a bathing suit, her swim cap tight on her head. The finishing touch to the whole look is a set of reflective goggles that look like they came straight from Michael Phelps's closet. As she turns to look at me, I spot what she's holding.

"Are you drinking straight out of the carton again?"

She hides the milk behind the refrigerator door, but there's a thin white line above her lip.

"You saw nothing!"

We both start laughing. It's so distracting that I don't notice Mom slipping through the doorway behind me. The sound of her voice actually makes me jump. "What on earth?"

Grammy stares back, goggles glinting. "What on earth, yourself."

"Are you trying out for the Olympics?"

I bust out laughing again. Grammy scowls.

"I take an underwater aerobics class!"

Mom nods. "You look like you're from the future."

I laugh again as Mom pretends to shield her eyes to get

past Grammy. I'm waiting for her to ask me what I've been up to—or if we went on a walk—but she's too distracted by the back and forth with Grammy. She plunks down on the couch as Grammy returns to her room, citing harassment by the "so-called fashion police." Mom opens a book and gestures for me to join her.

I snag my own book from the unread pile we keep stacked in one corner. She smiles at me from across the couch. "Thanks for working so hard today, honey."

We sit there in silence, reading our separate books, and at first I'm smiling about everything. I really can't believe I did it. A month's worth of homework, saving Jeffrey, the works.

Just another Saturday in the life of Celia Cleary.

And then that thought hits me. Like a punch to the gut.

How long can I really keep this up?

CHAPTER EIGHTEEN

The Martian

A whole day passes without another vision.

I wake up early Monday morning and make some cherry blossom tea. Nothing happens. I frown as I get ready for school. Usually I see something by now. I try not to let those thoughts distract me during the first few periods of school. After all, I made a promise to Mom that I need to keep. Any leftover time in class goes to getting ahead on homework. When I turn in my packet full of completed work to Mrs. Honea, she looks relieved.

"Back on the right track. Good work, Celia."

Lunch is relaxing for once. No plotting out how to save Jeffrey. Instead, I sit in the courtyard with DeSean and Sophie, debating the positives and negatives of a trip to Mars. The first astronauts to be selected to train for the interplanetary mission were announced, and the Courtyard Kids have basically been buzzing about it all week. Sophie is really excited.

"Four of the five astronauts are women," she says. "If there was a rocket ship waiting in the parking lot, I would board right now. Mars is off to a much better start than Earth."

DeSean shakes his head. "Have you ever seen *Alien*? Or *The Graviators*? There's a reason people always die in those movies! Space is *literally* trying to kill you. Couldn't pay me to go to Mars."

I'm about to mention one of the safety statistics I read the other day when I sense someone hovering to our right. I look over in surprise. It's Jeffrey Johnson.

"Hey. Is this seat free?" he asks.

None of us respond right away because *what on earth is happening?* DeSean and Sophie stare at him like he actually came from Mars. My brain struggles to send actual words for me to speak. I manage to point a finger at the open seat before stuttering out a mangled version of two separate words.

"Surehere. Here. Sure."

He sits. What. Is. Happening?

"Hey. I'm Jeffrey."

He offers a hand to Sophie. She and DeSean both introduce themselves, even though I'm pretty sure that Jeffrey and DeSean have a few classes together. I glance around the rest of the courtyard. Jeffrey's soccer hoodie might as well be a red flag. He's increased our athlete count from zero to one just by showing up. I look back at Jeffrey in time to see him pointing a fry at me.

"I live down the street from Celia."

DeSean nods. Sophie glances my way, and I can see her obvious concern. Which I totally understand. Sophie doesn't know the whole story with Avery. She thinks it was cheerleading camp and Jordan Lyles who stole our best friend away. She doesn't know my family's magic was the main issue.

"I heard you talking about Mars," Jeffrey says. "Mars is a jerk."

Sophie stares at him. "A what?"

"It's a book," Jeffrey clarifies. "I read it last year. *Mars Is a Jerk*. It's by one of my favorite YouTubers. Basically talks about all the reasons that Mars is a huge jerk. Like the fact that there are temperature shifts of over a hundred degrees in the same day."

"See?" DeSean jumps in. "Even if space doesn't kill you, Mars will."

Sophie rolls her eyes. "If I can handle Mrs. Bonner's classroom, I can handle Mars."

We all laugh. Mrs. Bonner's room is notorious. Always below sixty degrees. The topic swings back to the atmosphere on Mars, and I'm amazed how easily Jeffrey falls in with our group. I can tell Sophie's still eyeing him with suspicion, but as I listen to him talk, it's easy to see that he's more than just another soccer kid walking around in a hoodie. He's kind of nerdier than we are. At the end of lunch, Jeffrey surprises us again.

"It's so nice out here. Can I sit with you guys tomorrow?"

DeSean nods like it's no big deal. Sophie considers him for a long second.

"Only if you quit calling us *guys*. Gender Recognition 101. Every time you refer to a mixed group as *guys*, you're giving that group the dominant status. It also ghosts the other group."

Sophie taught me the same lesson earlier this year. Jeffrey blinks once before nodding.

"Oh. Right. Yeah. I can do that."

"Perfect," Sophie says. "And text me a link to that Mars book. Catch you later."

And just like that, Jeffrey's been accepted into our group. DeSean jogs after Sophie, who's basically bulldozing her way through the gathered crowds in the hallway.

Jeffrey raises an eyebrow at me. "How am I supposed to text her?"

I laugh. "I have her number."

He hands me his phone. I swipe through to the contacts.

"You could add yours in there too."

My stomach actually does a backflip. An Olympic-level, through-the-air backflip. I glance up from the phone to find Jeffrey carefully avoiding eye contact, his cheeks vaguely red. He looks back after a second and shrugs.

"Just so I can text you the link to the Mars book too. If you want."

For some reason, I feel like I'm sweating. Am I sweating? My fingers struggle to find the right keys. It takes way too long to enter both of our numbers in the phone. I don't make direct eye contact as I hand it back to him. Why does all this feel so awkward?

I start walking toward class, and Jeffrey walks beside me.

It's like he *wants* to walk with me? Here at school?

It takes a moment to realize that I now live in a world where Jeffrey and I walk places together. It's so strange and new that I'm expecting other people to stop and ask us what's going on. No one does, though, because it's really not *that* weird. Everyone is walking somewhere with someone. This is totally normal. Totally normal. We make the turn into the 1700 hallway, shoulders almost touching a few times, and I finally spot someone who *is* watching us.

Avery.

She's at the end of the hallway, filling up her water bottle. I see a brief glimpse of her in the park, crying over Jordan Lyles. And then another glimpse of her in the same park, shouting at me for something I didn't even do. She watches me—walking step for step with Jeffrey—and a single breath passes where I feel bad for being happy when I know she's sad. And then she whips away from the water fountain and around the corner without looking back.

CHAPTER NINETEEN

A Family Vision

A strangely perfect week follows.

I keep waking up and thinking the next vision of Jeffrey's death will come, only it doesn't. I also keep waiting for the day when Jeffrey will get bored of sitting with us in the courtyard. As if one day he's going to just stand up and walk back to his soccer friends. But then I remember the vision where I walked behind them through the woods, listening to a conversation that never actually happened. It seemed like Jeffrey was an outsider still. Someone who was trying to fit in, but hadn't quite found his place. Having him in *our* group is like a new instrument joining our orchestra. Kind of like he's figured out the kind of music we like to play and he's hopping into the song with us.

Mom ungrounds me after a series of emails from Mrs. Honea that confirm I'm back on the right track with my grades. Sophie officially starts a protest about the clothing restrictions for our upcoming field trip to Jungle Rapids. She wants the principal to correct the dress code on the forms so that it's equal for the boys and the girls. We show up one morning for the first organizational meeting. Even with the tempting offer of doughnuts, our crew and Jeffrey are the only ones who end up attending. For some reason, that feels like the moment he becomes a real member of our group. Sophie's approval always goes a long way.

There's even one morning when Avery sees me at the bus stop and whispers a quiet "Good morning." I'm so shocked that I don't even know what to say. My whole plan has been to use my magic for good, and eventually show Avery that she was wrong about Grammy, and magic. I wanted to have a few successes under my belt so that I could really explain what it is we do. But saving Jeffrey over and over again has sidetracked everything.

I know she's seen me hanging out with Jeffrey more. And I've seen her and Jordan standing as far from each other as possible at the bus stop. A part of me wonders if she just wants to talk now because everything fell apart with him? Grammy always says people deserve second chances, but she never really specified how quickly you have to give them out.

The highlight of the week comes on Friday. Grammy gets a phone call that has her hooting and laughing like she's a kid again. I pause my homework, eavesdropping as best I can, until she hangs up and turns a sly smile in our direction.

"Hope the two of you are ready for a rowdy weekend. Your cousins are going to stop by on their way down to Florida. That was your Aunt Corabel."

I can't help grinning. "Martha and Mary? You better hide the sodas."

Grammy grins back. Both cousins are several years older than I am, which means they've had their prophetic gifts longer. Last time they visited, both girls kept sneaking sodas in an effort to heighten their sixth sense, all so they could cheat at Monopoly. Except the two of them started trying to cheat against each other and ended up in a shouting match that woke up half the neighborhood. I guess it didn't help that Grammy, Mom, and I were laughing hysterically the whole time.

I'm sent upstairs to prepare the guest bedroom. Mom heads to the store with an unnecessarily long grocery list. Grammy spends the rest of the day baking up buckeye cookies and all the other little treats she knows my cousins love. My aunt Corabel is all business. She'll probably be flying down the highway and telling the girls the car won't stop until it stops for good.

After the bed is made and the towels are set out, I head downstairs and start making a cup of cherry blossom tea. It's been a full six days without even a hint of a vision. In some of the previous deaths, the tea helped resummon the vision for examination purposes.

I'm starting to get a little nervous about it now. A little hopeful, too.

Grammy occasionally looks up from her baking as my tea boils, but doesn't say anything. I take the cup over to the living room, sipping carefully, but after half an hour nothing happens. Mom bustles back through with groceries and asks me to help unload. I take advantage of Mom ducking into the bathroom to bring up the subject to Grammy.

"I haven't had another vision."

She's kneading dough. "Oh?"

"It's been almost a week."

She glances over. "It will come."

I feel a familiar frustration. It's almost like she wants another vision to come. "What if I stopped it? I'm pretty sure I've changed his future at this point. Kind of a lot."

Grammy raises an eyebrow. "Saving him changes a lot of futures. That's the lesson I've been hoping you'd see, Celia. What happens if you save him from one death? But the next death involves even more people? This is fickle work. Anything can happen."

Her answer doesn't help. "I can't just let it happen. Not now."

Those words catch Grammy's attention.

"Oh? And what has changed?"

I was kind of hoping to keep this part a secret, partially because saying it out loud feels like bad luck. "Well, Jeffrey hangs out with us now."

Grammy's eyebrow manages to shoot up a little higher. "Does he?"

"Like at lunch. And on the bus. I was saving him before because . . . it felt right. To save him. I don't know. It feels right to save anyone who's in danger and doesn't know it. But now it's kind of different. I've gotten to know Jeffrey. He's really smart. Kind of nerdy. I went to one of his soccer games the other day. He plays defense. I think. I don't know. He's kind of . . . great."

"Great," she repeats. "Like he's a talented mathematician with a bright future?"

I laugh at that. "No, Grammy. Like he's nice, I guess. And funny."

She returns to kneading the dough. It's not like she's ignoring me, because she's got that same face she always has when I ask her some deep and meaningful question, like she's reading the whole universe and trying to translate it back to me. Her voice is quiet when she speaks.

"So you like him."

The words have me blushing. I mean, of course I *like* him. And I kind of *like like* him too. Jeffrey is really nice to talk to and he's fun to be around and that's all there is to it. Before Grammy can say more, though, Mom comes back into the room.

"Don't worry," she says. "I already hid Monopoly."

We laugh. There's about twenty more minutes of quiet preparation. Mom plays some music. Grammy hums along. I clean the dishes as Grammy bakes, and it's one of those rare moments of peace in our busy house. A second later, my cousins burst through the door without even knocking.

"Told you she was going to make buckeyes!" Martha shouts triumphantly. She shoulders past Mary, who rolls her eyes in annoyance. It's been long enough that I notice the changes right away. Martha wears more makeup than

I remember. But it's Mary who is completely transformed. She's always been tall, but now she's layered some muscle over her skinny frame. Her hair's almost blond. Not unnaturally. Just colored from being out in the sun.

Martha heads straight for the desserts. Mary heads straight for me.

"How's the family's newest seer?" she asks with a smile.

It's been so stressful saving Jeffrey that sometimes I forget I'm a part of this secret and ancient club, a club that Mom will never get to join, one that's passed down through generations.

"Doing just fine," I say, giving her a hug. "What the heck happened to you? Are you training for a marathon or something?"

Mary smiles, always so polite. "It's nothing much. I joined the rowing team. It's really nice. I needed it more for up here, really." She taps the side of her head. "Rowing isn't about predictions or probabilities. Either we win or we lose. I needed some part of my life to not be about the prophecy stuff, you know?"

I've only had my gift for about three weeks, but I totally get it.

"Definitely."

Somehow Mom and Aunt Corabel already have glasses of wine in hand. Grammy's fussing over Martha, who sweeps me into a hug while Mary sneaks a few buckeye cookies. We eventually make our way to the kitchen table. Grammy starts churning out grilled cheeses. We sip at soup and laugh at stories, and it's the best kind of reunion.

"Enough about us," Mary finally says. "Celia had her first vision, right? Do tell."

The whole room reacts to the request in very different ways. Mom reaches for her wine. Aunt Corabel has a familiar forced smile on her face. Martha starts banging her fists on the table excitedly, and Grammy watches me with a mix of pride and curiosity. It takes me a second to figure out how to tell the truth without freaking Mom out.

"The first one was tricky," I reply. "So was the second. And the third. And the tenth. I've learned to use a little cherry blossom tea. And my magical scent is campfire."

Martha shakes her head. "Lucky! Mary gets waffle cones. You get campfires. Every time I glimpse something, it's basically like walking into that old-lady store Mom always made us visit in the mall. Remember, Mary? The one where you broke that chess set?"

Aunt Corabel frowns. "I thought you broke those, Martha?"

"She *did* break them," Mary says. "But she knew if she stood in just the right spot, she could blame it all on me. Always such a sneak."

Martha laughs. "Whatever. Mom figured out what I was trying to do. She made me use my own money to pay for it. Remember that chess set? It was so busted. The horses were taped together. I'm pretty sure we replaced one of the rooks with a battery or something. Besides, that's probably why my visions all smell like old-lady decorations. It's clearly a punishment."

Aunt Corabel launches into the defense of her favorite store. Grammy's listening to it all with a smile, but I notice that Mary is still watching me. She gives me a little wink, and I can't help wondering if she knows that I didn't exactly share the *whole* story about what's been going on.

The conversation moves on. Mom and Aunt Corabel clink their glasses. Grammy keeps placing new dishes and desserts on the table. We start setting up a game of Ultimate Catan until Mary lets out a little sigh.

"I'm sorry. Had too much sugar," she says. "We're going to roll a *lot* of nines and an abnormal amount of elevens. Let's play Scrabble instead?"

Martha laughs obnoxiously as she grabs the new game. I was there for both of their first visions. They used to live just an hour away. Moving out of state was the only reason they missed mine. It's hard to not feel a little jealous as I watch them. Mary's visions are all about probabilities. I remember Grammy saying that Martha sees auras. I kind of wish my visions were about what people felt or what kind of dice rolls we were going to have. Death feels like an unlucky specialization to have landed in.

We make it through four rounds before Mary accuses Martha of cheating.

"Of course I'm cheating," she complains. "Grammy's about to play something good. I can tell she's excited about the letters she's just got. And Celia's got enough vowels to start a basketball team. Pretty sure she's pulled four *E*s in a row. Not exactly helping me, though, is it?"

Grammy has the high score. Martha sits in dead last.

My cousin smiles as she sets out her word. *L-O-S-E-R.*

"Just five points."

When Grammy's lead is out of reach, we decide to call it a night. Our moms are laughing loudly in the living room, telling random stories. Mom has always been close to Aunt Corabel. They're both really different people, but they share the bond of being the unmagical parents of magical children. It's nice to see her laughing so much with someone.

I show Martha and Mary up to their room and then start getting ready for bed. I'm smiling to myself, thankful for a distracting night, when the sisters come storming into my room. Both of them are dressed in comfy clothes. Martha leaps onto the bed next to me.

"Did you really think you were going to get away with *that* explanation?" she asks.

Mary smiles as she sits down on the edge of the bed. "We know how hard it was for our mom at first. It's not easy to talk about all the details. But *we* want to know. How's everything *really* going, Celia? Give us all the juicy details."

I take a deep breath. Grammy knows most of it, but she's been against saving Jeffrey since the start. Maybe the sisters will have some ideas. I decide to tell them *everything*. All the details of the first vision. Tricking construction workers and making fake calls to park deputies. Every detail of how I've saved Jeffrey over and over again. I end by telling them about the Crab Shack.

Even Grammy doesn't know about that one.

"The more I save him," I say quietly, "the more I like him. He's really nice."

Martha snuggles a little closer to me. She reads auras, so I'd guess she can tell just how upset I am about everything. "It's not the easiest first vision to have," she says.

Mary asks, "And Grammy didn't have any solutions?"

I shake my head. "She said there are two rules. Everyone dies, and fate chooses."

"Very uplifting," Martha replies.

"Right? It's nice to talk to both of you about it. Thanks for listening."

Mary nods. "You haven't talked with anyone else?"

I shrug. "I wasn't sure if we're allowed to? Besides, talking about my magical gifts didn't seem like the best way to make friends. I'm already weird enough as it is."

Martha smacks my arm. "Weird is good. Trust me."

Mary is far gentler. "It's okay to tell the *right* people. Grammy did that. She's told a few of her best friends over the years. Most people just laugh it off. Pretend like you're messing with them or something. But the people who really know you? They've usually sensed something was different all along. And they'll stick with you. No matter what."

An image of DeSean and Sophie appears in my mind. I've felt so alone over the past few weeks. Saving Jeffrey with only Grammy's disapproving voice in my head. It'd be kind of nice to have friends like them helping me out. But then a flash of Avery's angry expression appears, and I wonder if it's worth the risk of losing them. Pretty sure that'd make this the worst year in history.

In the quiet that follows, Mary's attention roams over to my desk. Random textbooks are scattered there, but I finally see what she's seeing: the Cleary Family Guide Book.

"We could help you," she says. "Fresh eyes!"

When I nod, Martha rolls off the side of the bed to retrieve the dusty old book. Mary crawls across the bed to snuggle in beside me. Martha rejoins us, and I instinctively open to the page in question. Both of them start reading the words that I've practically memorized by now.

"There's something here about a trade . . . ," Martha reads.

"Doesn't stop the death," Mary points out. "It just gives the vision to a different seer. Besides, I'm guessing Celia already thought about that one."

I nod. "Definitely. It would just give the vision to someone who cares less about saving Jeffrey than I do. Not a great recipe for keeping him alive."

Martha turns the page dramatically. "Maybe there's an

answer in the Catalyst section? Most of us just see and react, right? Catalysts can bend fate, though. . . ."

"Wait," Mary says. "Go back."

Martha sighs and turns the page. We both watch Mary trace the bottom line very carefully. She mouths the words in a barely audible whisper. "Turn the page again."

"Great work, Sherlock," Martha says.

Mary's focused, though. She keeps reading the line and I read along with her, allowing myself at least a little bit of hope for once. When she's done, she stabs a finger down to the bottom-right corner. "No wonder you're having a hard time."

"What?" I sit up straighter. "Why? What do you mean?"

"There's a page missing."

Mary points to the bottom of the page. The numerical system is something ancient that I wasn't really paying close attention to at all. She moves Martha's hand and turns the page back to the first one in the section. "The sentence here doesn't lead to the sentence on the next page. It's nonsense. It doesn't line up. And that's because there's an entire page missing. Look at the numbers. It skips."

My heart is pounding in my chest. "There's a missing page."

The death section has a missing page. Which means there's actually a chance. There might be information somewhere that really could save Jeffrey. But that hopeful thought leads to a less hopeful one. "Where would it be?"

Mary presses the pages together and runs her finger down the binding. "No idea. It's a really clean tear, but this book is old as dirt. Some of my old books lose pages like this all the time. The bindings get loose and they just slip out. That could have happened."

"Or someone took it out," Martha suggests. "Maybe the information was too dangerous?"

The two of them throw theories back and forth, but my mind has taken a direct road to what feels like the most obvious answer. There's one person who was entrusted to care for this book and has had it in her possession for decades now. It's hard to believe that she'd be the one responsible, but the clues all lead to her.

"Grammy."

CHAPTER TWENTY

The Art of Confrontation

A big breakfast waits downstairs in the morning.

Our moms have exchanged wineglasses for coffee mugs. I kind of love to see them leaning together like conspirators in a heist. Maybe they're discussing their strange children. Or maybe they're talking about work. I'm not sure, but it's nice to see them creating their own fun together, even if it's only for a morning. Grammy is busy making pancakes.

Martha stabs into the first stack with her fork. "The famous pancakes!"

"Legendary," Mary agrees. "Are we old enough to know the secret ingredient yet?"

Grammy turns a smile our way. I'm so used to her pancakes that I'd forgotten they were famous with the rest of the family. I'm also still stuck on the clue I learned last night. The missing page in the family spell book.

A part of me wants to be mad at Grammy. A part of me is suspicious she's hiding something. Another part wonders if I'm just wrong about it all. Maybe the page was ripped out a long time ago. I've been wrong before. A lot of times, actually.

"The secret ingredient?" Grammy smiles. "I suppose you're old enough. The secret ingredient is three teaspoons of unconditional love. Best added as a powder, though if all you have is the bottled kind . . ."

Mary throws a balled-up napkin in Grammy's direction that falls well short. Martha actually boos her. "I'm going to college soon," she says, pointing her fork. "If I could make these?! Everyone would love me. . . ."

Mary nods knowingly. "You'd rule the school. I can see it now. The Queen of Wake Forest."

"Don't worry," Martha says, making her voice sound British. "I will be a just queen."

"I do not doubt that," Grammy replies, setting down another stack. "For now, I'd like my queens well fed. Eat up. Your mother wants to hit the road after breakfast."

True to form, Corabel sweeps to her feet the second her daughters' plates are clean. Mom sets down her mug with a heavy sigh, but she smiles when Corabel delivers a huge hug. Mary and Martha have adopted some of their mother's efficiency, because both of them are packed and out by their car before I can even blink.

All three of them hug Grammy goodbye, planting kisses on both cheeks. Watching them, it hits me that I've gotten used to Grammy. We go on walks together. We cook side by side most nights. She watches shows with me, or reads the same books. I realize this is a brief taste for them of what's become normal for me. And some days I act like it's not the greatest thing in the world.

My heart sings a little. I'm still not sure what to make of the missing page, but I'm really lucky to have Grammy in a way they haven't. Martha wraps a quick arm around my neck and kisses my forehead. She pulls back long enough to smile. "You're a brighter color this morning. Looks good on you, kid. It'll all turn out okay."

Mary steps forward next. She leans in to hug me, and there's a whisper of a second where only I can hear her voice. The words she speaks are so bold and unexpected that I have to stop myself from gasping out loud.

"He's in a lot of the futures I see," she whispers. "But not all of them."

The hope in the first half of her prediction is swept off by the doubt cast by the second. I know Mary sees probabilities—hundreds and hundreds of futures. The idea that Jeffrey can *actually* survive is thundering through my chest. She offers a sympathetic look before slipping into the back seat of the car. I'm still barely breathing as Martha leans across her to wave.

Aunt Corabel honks the horn, waiting just long enough for them to close their doors before rumbling up the street. I stand there huddled with Mom in the slight cold of the morning, and watch the car grow smaller. Mom says something about retrieving her coffee.

When I look back, I find Grammy watching me. She always seems to know what I'm thinking. Her voice is calm and quiet. "We should go on a walk together."

There's a sentence hiding behind those words: *We have a lot to talk about.* Mom calls back to us from the porch. "Bundle up before you go. I've got running club in an hour."

Grammy's smile widens, like she knew she'd have me all to herself. Now I can't help wondering exactly what she knows. I nod to her. "Sure, I'd love to go for a walk."

I'm trying to act mysterious, but one corner of my heart just wants a taste of normal. Before I had any visions. Before I knew what was going to happen to Jeffrey Johnson. Grammy and I used to walk down the greenway just to walk. There were no mysteries in the air between us. We walked together because it felt good to move through the world with someone we loved.

Knowing it'll be a little colder on the shaded greenway, I throw on a comfy sweater that's jammed into the back of the shoe closet. I'm pulling the thing overhead when I remember that Jeffrey likes to run through the park in the morning. I consider the sweater's endless wrinkles.

Maybe I'm paranoid, but it also kind of smells? I set it aside and fish through the closet for something else to wear. Grammy's already wrapped up and ready to go when I turn back to her.

She offers a playful smile. "I doubt he'd have noticed the smell, even if we ran into him."

It's annoying how well she knows me. I don't even think she had to use magic to figure out the reason for why I'm not wearing my normal sweater.

"Zip it!" I whisper back, but I can't help smiling.

We take a left out the front door. Our row of houses is tucked right against the greenway. We take another left and cross a wooden bridge that jumps the creek, and it's like stepping into a new world. The sound of passing cars fades. An occasional plane passes overhead, but I've always loved how peaceful it is back here. Grammy links her arm in mine. We sidestep as a biker comes shooting past.

Her favorite tree is ahead on our left. It has cast a spray of flowers onto the walk below. My favorite looms up on the right, its neck craned down like it's drinking from the pond.

Grammy leads us quietly on. Jeffrey Johnson makes no appearance, which has me feeling a little silly about the wardrobe change. Eventually she breaks the silence.

"You have a question for me."

We're passing the pond as she says it. The water reflects the brightening sky. I turn to look at her and can't help smiling. "How do you always know?"

"It's a blessing and a curse," she replies. "Out with it."

I spent half the night trying to figure out the best way to approach the subject, but there's no such thing as a plan of attack with Grammy. She already knows most of the moves I want to make.

"There's a page missing in the Cleary Family Guide Book."

Grammy nods. "There are several pages missing, actually. But that isn't a question."

I'm kind of thankful for how direct she's being. It has me feeling a little less bad about asking the questions I actually want to ask. "Who ripped it out?"

"I'm sure you have a guess."

That almost makes me snort. "Fine. You ripped it out."

She nods. "You are correct."

I didn't expect it to be that easy. An admission of guilt. I was *actually* right. There's a brief taste of victory, but that leads straight to anger. I didn't *want* to be right. It's been exhausting trying to keep Jeffrey alive. I've asked Grammy for help all along, and she just kept telling me it wasn't possible. But now she's admitting that she kept important information from me.

It means that she lied.

"You didn't tell me the truth."

"In a way," she replies. "But there is—as always—more to the story."

I have to bite my tongue. It's not fair. Adults always seem to have an excuse. It's kind of like they get to do what they want and as long as they have a fancy argument, they can get away with it. That's never worked for me. I don't want her to explain it away. I just want to know how to save Jeffrey once and for all.

Grammy begins. "As you know, my gift is with psychometry. It is the art of viewing important future events through objects. Long ago, I had a premonition by accident. I was thirty years old at the time, and your mother was just a little girl. You weren't even alive. Not then. It was just a glimpse; that's how most of my visions happen. I do not see the full picture the way you do. Generally, I see important pieces of a larger picture. It's almost like seeing something symbolic. And I've gotten quite good at working the clues out after all these years."

She hesitates, but only briefly.

"On that day, I was reading the family guide book. When I arrived at that page, the touch of my fingers to those words stirred a vision. I was plunged briefly underwater. I couldn't breathe. It's hard to explain now, but I knew that vision could end in the death of a loved one. I knew that the danger would come many years down the road. I knew it would be someone within our family, as the vision was created by the guide book itself, which only our family can access. And I knew that it would be specific to what was on that page. One of my grandchildren would be in grave danger if I did not act."

I don't ask for her to explain how she could know all that from one glimpse. I know what she means from experience. It would be hard to explain my visions to someone else. I'm sure her magic is the same way.

"My sister had a talent for tracing magic," she continues. "Linking one event to another. It took a great deal of time to measure out the consequences of our actions. What would happen if we ripped the page out? What would happen if we left it there? Should we burn the page, or bury it in the woods just in case the information would be valuable later? All four siblings worked on this together. It took time, but eventually we all agreed to tear the page out of the journal. Our hope was that taking action would save the life of a loved one."

I frown, turning over the pieces of what she's said, examining each one. It's hard to pick which question I should ask first. When I don't speak, Grammy goes on.

"Do you understand, Celia? The information is out of reach."

I ball my hands into fists.

"No way, Grammy. I know you. You'd never forget a single word on that page."

She flashes a proud smile, as if she's honored by my words. "Correct again. I do not forget anything . . . which is why I never read the page in question. We divided the tasks. My oldest sister—Patricia—was the one who read the contents. I have always suspected that the information had something to do with death visions, given its location in the book. I am also certain, now, that it contained relevant information to what you're experiencing with Jeffrey. But that information was also life-endangering, Celia. I never read a word of it."

For a moment, we look at each other. A part of me wonders if she's lying. It wouldn't be the first time. I'm holding my breath, hoping this is all a big joke.

"Your sister, the one who read it . . ."

"She passed away twelve years ago."

I knew that two of Grammy's siblings had passed away. My great-aunt—Susie—lives down in Texas. Grammy doesn't talk about her very often. Grammy once remarked that Susie spends more time shooting at rabbits than using her gifts. I was hoping she was the one who read the page. That I might still have access to it. My frustration is reaching a boiling point.

"So there's no one alive that knows the answer?"

"Correct."

She answers without hesitation. Her eyes don't dart away. She doesn't fumble with her hands. None of the suspicious actions that might suggest a lie. I watch her for a second longer, and it feels like she's telling the truth. It's a small relief to know she isn't guilty of intentionally sabotaging me. But that feeling is quickly overshadowed as I put the pieces together.

"Your vision was about me," I say, working out the logic slowly. "And you took the page out of the book to save me from whatever I would have done if I'd read that page."

Which means there *was* something important written

there, even if it was dangerous. Grammy nods. "The future is always so complicated. What we do is never perfect, because life itself is imperfect. One choice echoes into other choices. I did my best, Celia. Ill omens hovered above a member of my family. At the time, you did not exist. I had no way of knowing it would be you. All I knew was that someone I would come to love was in danger. We removed the page to keep you safe, and I can only hope that removing that page was *enough* to keep you safe."

I speak the truth she's not saying out loud.

"But saving me may have doomed Jeffrey."

Grammy makes a gesture with her free hand. It's one I've learned over the years. Her way of saying that no one could know, not even a seer like her. She looks so helpless.

"Oh, Celia. I'm so sorry. You are at the very beginnings of your power. So far you have only seen very direct cause and effect. Saving Jeffrey's life delays death. Death picks a new fate for him. You delay it again. But so much of our magic is more complicated than that. Even the slightest nudges from us can change the world."

I frown. "Like your nudge to Mrs. Sumner?"

It's the first time that Grammy looks surprised. I never intended to bring up Avery's mom, but for some reason, the idea of a slight nudge changing someone's world made me think of her. That was Avery's big accusation, after all. That Grammy's advice is the reason her parents decided to split up.

"Mrs. Sumner?"

"That's Avery's mom," I say quietly. "Avery told me that her mom came to see you. She wanted advice on her marriage. And a few weeks later, Avery's parents split up. I know you would never intentionally hurt someone . . . but . . ."

Grammy shakes her head. "Mrs. Sumner did come to see me. I performed my usual magic. I promise, Celia, that I did not tell Mrs. Sumner anything she didn't already know."

"I know you didn't," I say. "But Avery thinks that's what happened. She said you were a fake. And then told me I was a freak if I believed in magic. I thought I could change her mind. If I was able to do some good things with my own visions, maybe she'd see . . ."

Grammy sees me breaking and does what she always does. It's not magic, not really, it's just her wrapping me up in her arms. The scent of her sweater and the press of my head to her shoulder.

"I'm so sorry, dear. There are always misunderstandings. I can only tell you that these things have a way of working themselves out. We cannot control how the world sees us. All we can do is use our magic to the best of our ability. We must be wise and gracious and kind. It is the only way to make the future a better place. I'm sorry, honey. Avery will understand as she grows older. I promise you. My magic did not break them up. She'll see that."

I nod into her shoulder, not trusting myself to speak without crying.

"All of this is hard," Grammy says. "I know it must be hard. Dealing with friendships. Saving Jeffrey over and over again. I want to be very clear about one thing." She pulls back to get a better look. I've been so caught up in my own emotions that I didn't notice that Grammy's sweet eyes are brimming with tears. "I am so immensely proud of the young girl you've become. I have thought about my decision to remove that page for decades. At least a few times a year. I didn't know then which grandchild I hoped to save by my actions. But I promise that I would make that decision a thousand times over, Celia. If it meant keeping you safe . . ."

It takes effort to set aside my anger. At least for a moment. Grammy is crying. As I look into her eyes, I see the same thing I saw earlier. A bright soul that loves me. It's not hard to sweep forward and wrap both my arms around her again. Her voice is a whisper in my ear.

"You are so wonderful," she says. "I never thought I would . . . admire you so much. You got the best parts of me. All the things I cherish, you've taken them and started to make them your own. What a difficult thing, dear. It's truly remarkable. I do not know everything, but I do know this: you have so very much ahead of you."

And now I'm trying not to cry again. It takes a lot of blinking to fight off the tears. I'm also trying not to mention the obvious problem with what she's saying.

Jeffrey Johnson has so very much ahead of him too.

Doesn't he? Isn't that the whole point of saving him?

I don't speak those words. This moment belongs to us. It's between Grammy and me. A quiet reminder that she's not the enemy, that she never was. We're on the same team.

"You're not so bad yourself," I finally say, pulling back to grin at her. "Stubborn is all."

A laugh jolts out of her. She ropes an arm back through mine and starts leading us back down the path. Everything isn't fixed. It is far from perfect. I'm still not sure what to do about Jeffrey. If Grammy expects me to stop saving him, she's going to be really disappointed.

But for just a moment, I walk beside her and pretend we're back on the 4,443rd day of my life. I pretend we're walking just to feel the breeze on our skin, and to enjoy that first scent of honeysuckle in the air. We walk on like that for a while.

It feels nice, even if it can't last.

CHAPTER TWENTY-ONE

Interrupted

Another week passes without a whisper of the future.

I want to let myself believe it's over, but I keep hearing the words Grammy last spoke about Jeffrey's next vision. *It will come.* Pretty much a promise from the lips of a seer. I'm stuck between believing somehow this could all be over, and knowing Grammy is right.

It has me tiptoeing through each day like someone walking through a field in a storm, hoping that lightning won't strike. Grammy used to say that if you spend too much time preparing for one danger, it leaves you vulnerable to other dangers.

Friday seems eager to prove her theory.

Jeffrey is walking with me. We always walk together after lunch now. Right as we reach his classroom, he hands me a note. An actual pen-and-paper note. I've only seen people write these on TV shows. My cheeks turn instantly red, even though the folded exterior just says:

To Celia

"I drew that for you in second period." He shrugs, as if this is normal. I look down and realize his hands are trembling slightly. "See you on the bus."

He turns so fast that he almost decks Cynthia Parker. He mumbles an awkward apology before vanishing into his classroom. It is the most hilarious and adorable thing I've ever seen. I unfold the note.

Jeffrey's a surprisingly good artist. Clearly better than I am. There's a comic version of him standing on a ladder by the door to the classroom. He's reaching up to turn the hands of the clock so that the school day will be over. I turn the note over, frowning. I thought it was going to be something sweet? I study the drawing again and it finally clicks.

The small version of Jeffrey hasn't turned the clock to 2:18, which is when the bell normally rings to let us out of school. He's turned the miniature hands to 2:34. A smile spreads across my face. The kind of smile where your cheeks almost start to hurt. That's right around the time every day that the two of us get off the bus together.

It's official.

I have a crush on Jeffrey Johnson.

When school ends, I head straight for the bus. I kind of love that the other kids have stopped taking the seat across from me, because they know Jeffrey will ask to sit there if they do. He grins his way down the aisle. We talk about nothing and everything, and it finally feels like some curse has lifted. I find myself checking the air around him, trying to see if those black threads are still there, eager to claim him, but there's nothing. Nothing but the two of us.

Jeffrey skips past his street, walking me all the way down to the townhouse. He does this most days, like he's trying to squeeze a few more minutes out of the day. It's a real surprise, though, when he stops and points to our front door for the first time ever.

"So your grandma tells fortunes or something?"

My entire body freezes in place. It's not exactly a secret. There's a sign for Grammy's business hanging on the front door. It's been there for as long as I've been alive. Sophie and DeSean have seen it, but like most people, they just assume it's a bizarre hobby. Mary and Martha said I should talk to someone about our magic, but I'm pretty sure they didn't mean I should talk to the boy I'm saving over and over again.

I consider my words carefully. "She's kind of an advice coach."

It feels like a betrayal. Grammy isn't a life coach. She's a powerful seer who comes from a line of powerful seers. And so am I. Jeffrey nods like that makes sense, and it stings a little to have to hide who we are. I'm kind of hoping he'll just drop the subject.

Which makes his next question even more of a lightning strike.

"Want to watch TV or something?"

My heart does some kind of acrobatic jump kick against my ribs. I'm staring at him and trying to remember how to speak when he finally sees the look on my face.

"I mean, we don't have to—I was just—"

My hands are literally sweating.

"Uhh. It's—I just have to get started on my homework."

He looks briefly disappointed, and I have no idea how to tell him that it's not that I don't *want* to hang out with him. It's just that Jeffrey has been the main topic of conversation between Grammy and me for weeks now. I've told her so much about him. If he walked in the door right now, it would be a disaster. Two worlds colliding in the most awkward way possible.

"Same here," he says, smiling like it's no big deal. "Catch you later, Cleary."

And my heart melts a little at the way he calls me

"Cleary." He starts walking back up the street, soccer cleats bouncing off his backpack. I make my way up the steps. I'm reaching for the door when the smell of campfire comes bursting forward.

"No, no, no . . ."

My hand barely clutches the handle as the smell floods in around me. I slip slightly, going down on one knee, before my vision of the world is ripped away. . . .

Jeffrey.

I'm standing in front of him. He smiles at me. Everything around him is black and empty. It's like he's standing on a Hollywood set that will have to be digitally altered later. Several details reach my brain, almost in slow motion. He's wearing a red hoodie. He's holding a paper that's crinkled. The words on his hoodie are hand-drawn. The message says something about *Star Wars*?

I've been on the lookout for this vision all week, so I hungrily step forward. I'm waiting for the scene to color in around him, but something *shoves* me away. A scent like dying flowers floods the air as the entire scene—including Jeffrey—vanishes from sight.

I'm back on the front stoop. Down on my knees. Struggling to breathe.

My heartbeat is racing.

No, no, no.

The vision is gone.

CHAPTER TWENTY-TWO

Bewitched

It takes effort to stand.

I feel like I've been running sprints up the stairs for hours. For some reason, the interrupted vision has taken a huge toll on me. It isn't supposed to happen like that. The closest comparison was with DeSean at school. He interrupted my vision, but as I look around the front porch, I see that the closest person is Mr. Hanes three doors down, mowing his lawn.

Why did the vision cut out?

After steadying my breathing, I turn the handle and

storm inside. Grammy's kneeling down by the oven. It almost looks like the same pose I was just in, except she's inspecting a batch of sugar cookies. I slam my backpack on the table. The noise draws her attention, and she throws a raised eyebrow in my direction.

"Celia?"

I ignore her question and head straight for the couch. A comfortable place. *Close your eyes. Draw on a distinct detail from within the vision.* I take my seat, shut my eyes, and imagine that red hoodie that Jeffrey was wearing. After one more exhale, I lean forward.

And I almost face-plant on the floor.

"Whoa!"

I catch myself just in time. It didn't work. Why didn't it work? I sit back on the couch and try again. *Focus, Celia. Focus.* All the same details. When I lean forward the second time, though, nothing happens again. I can't recall the vision. It's not even blinking briefly into existence. It's like the entire thing just *vanished*.

"Celia?"

I'm on the verge of tears. Grammy is standing off to the side.

"My vision," I gasp out. "The vision cut off. I couldn't see what happened."

Grammy considers that before nodding knowingly. There's a brief second where I'm mad that she always has the answers, but there's relief, too. Maybe her answers will help this time.

"That's in the family guide book. We discussed this at the beginning. There are diminishing returns to magic like this, Celia. Spend too much time using the same spell, pursuing the same subject, and the magic begins to dwindle. It cannot last forever."

I take another deep breath, trying to stop my hands from shaking.

"Tell me how to bring it back," I demand. "Tell me what to do."

She starts to shake her head before seeing the desperation on my face. If she doesn't help me, I can't figure out how he dies. I won't know where he dies either. I'll have no clues to help me stop the inevitable. Grammy finally relents.

"What did you see?"

I try to think back through everything. My brain feels scrambled, though, with a headache that's only getting worse. It felt like death itself shoved me out of the vision. Even the most basic details are getting fuzzier. It takes all my effort to recall the most central one.

"Red."

And that detail links itself to the next.

"He was wearing a red hoodie with writing on the front?" I frown. "He was holding a piece of paper, too. I couldn't see what it was. Maybe he was turning in worksheets? Maybe that means it will happen at school?"

Grammy thinks about those details before walking back into the kitchen. She rummages through her desk. For the first time, it feels like we're partners. Using magic to figure things out together. She returns with a box of colored pencils and a blank sheet of paper.

"Draw what you can remember. Every detail."

I'm not exactly Picasso, but I open the box. Grammy

doesn't explain the purpose of what I'm doing. She returns to the oven, humming the same song she always does when clients are about to visit. I remember the humming is a method she uses for focusing her own magic. It's a tune I've heard my entire life. She pulls out the freshly baked sugar cookies and sets them on the stovetop. I finish shading in Jeffrey's shirt. The red isn't quite the right color, but it's close enough. It takes about fifteen minutes to finish. Grammy is waiting with a cup of tea.

"Drink this."

She sets it down on the table in front of me. I take several sips. It has my head clearing almost immediately. I take a deeper sip before glancing at her. "What's in here?"

"Rosehips for clarity," she answers. "Have some more."

I set the drawing aside and keep sipping the tea. My headache slowly vanishes. Grammy brings down the Cleary Family Guide Book. I can't help feeling a little annoyed as I look at it. The book is full of magic. It's supposed to be my inheritance, but right now all I can think is that it's missing the one piece of information that might actually help me.

A page that was ripped out long ago.

Grammy finds what she's looking for. "Do you have anything from Jeffrey?"

On instinct, I shake my head, because that would be *so* creepy, but then I realize that I *do* have something he gave me. The note that he drew for me. I start digging through my book bag, flipping open folders, until the little folded rectangle slides out.

Grammy snatches the note. She heads to one of her cabinets, removes a very particular candle, and then selects a few herbs from the pantry. I watch her light the candle. After a few seconds, she sprinkles the herbs into the flame. The smell alters ever so slightly.

And then she lowers Jeffrey's drawing.

I practically shout the words, "Hey! That's mine!"

Grammy pauses, a little surprised. "Oh. Right. Well, it's . . . nice."

An awkward moment passes where we both look at each other. And then we're laughing. It's not funny. It really isn't. But some part of me is glad she was here to witness the first love letter I've ever received. And it's only natural that she's trying to burn it in order to perform a magical spell. It's such a Cleary thing to do that I can't even be mad at her.

"Do you have to?" I ask.

"It's a spell to retrieve a lost vision," Grammy explains. "This is the only trick that came to mind. I have no idea if it will work. We'll just have to wait and see. You have to burn the picture, turn the candle three times, then imagine the vision of Jeffrey. It might restore what you saw."

I take the drawing, shaking my head sadly. After a second, I lower it into the candle's flame. We watch a dark circle form at the center of the page, blossoming where the clock was. The fire spreads until the image distorts and the air starts to smell funny.

Grammy repeats the instructions. I sit down, turning the candle three times clockwise. On the final rotation, I let go of the candle and close my eyes, focusing on the image of Jeffrey standing in that dark dreamscape. A red hoodie. A message written on the front. Crumpled papers. It's a very different taste of magic. Nothing like my usual attempts.

When my cousins and I were little, we used to go to the pond near our house. We'd shove our hands into the water and run them along the bank. Digging and searching until our hands landed on quarter turtles. We'd take them home and make them pets. This feels a lot like that.

A hand stretching into the unknown, in search of a prize.

My eyes stay closed. The room is silent except for Grammy's humming. The dark doesn't flinch. No image of Jeffrey is restored into my vision. I find myself pleading desperately with the magic. *Just give me this vision. This one time. I won't let the next one get away.*

Grammy finally sets a hand on my shoulder. "Celia, I think—"

A knock sounds at the door.

We both jump. The candle is still burning. Jeffrey's note is a crumpled, black ball. I quickly hide my own drawing before walking over to the door. A glance through the eyehole has my head whipping back around, eyes wide. I whisper across the room.

"It's Jeffrey!"

Grammy bites her lip and shrugs, like this was all very unexpected. Nervously, I open the door. Jeffrey's wearing a strange expression, almost confused. "Hey. You wanted me?"

"Yes," I say before coming to my senses. "I mean. No? What?"

Jeffrey stares back, and it's clear something is going on with him. His eyes roam the inside of our house. He smiles suddenly. "You know, I've always wondered what it's like in here. . . ."

And without asking, he stumbles into the room.

I shoot a warning look at Grammy. She still looks a little shocked, though. I'm impressed by how quickly she smiles at Jeffrey, pretending this is all totally normal.

"I'm Celia's grandmother. And you are?"

"I'm Jeffrey," he replies. "I have a crush on Celia."

His words have me blushing violently. Grammy's eyes go wide, and she has to choke back a laugh. "Of course you do. I've made cookies. Want one?"

He nods. "I have soccer practice in an hour. I can eat two. If I eat three, I'll probably yack."

The honesty of everything he's saying is very alarming. Something is wrong. Grammy and I exchange another concerned glance as he plucks two cookies from the tray. She shoots me a *What happened?* look, and I try to shoot her a *You're the expert* look in return.

I know the spell brought him to the house, but is it also why he's answering everything so honestly? How is the magic working? Jeffrey turns around and catches us exchanging looks.

"You two have a secret?" He grins. "Don't worry. My mom taught me not to be nosy." He starts walking toward the couch in the living room, but pulls up short when he's right in front of me. He looks at me very carefully and says, "Speaking of nosy, the freckles on the bridge of your nose are adorable."

And then he keeps walking, sugar cookies in hand. We watch as he sits down on the couch like he's lived here for years. I almost laugh when he fishes through the cushion and somehow finds the remote. A few clicks and he's flipping through channels.

Grammy crosses the room to stand beside me, her voice a hissed whisper.

"I think the spell backfired."

"No kidding!"

Jeffrey seems unaware. "Want to watch *The Dread Files*? I can't watch it at home. My brother gets too scared and has nightmares. Also, this couch? Very comfortable. Great choice."

He doesn't wait for an answer, cueing up the show he mentioned. Another laugh almost jumps out of my throat. This is unbelievable. After a moment, I round on Grammy.

"You bewitched him," I accuse.

Grammy shakes her head. "Actually, you did! This is a spell to retrieve something lost. I guess you accidentally summoned Jeffrey, instead of the vision of him. You also must have put a little more oomph behind the magic, because it seems like you're also retrieving *information* from him. Pretty solid work for your first potion. . . ."

"Hey. No flattery allowed," I throw back in a whisper. "And what do you mean 'summoned him'? He's not a golden retriever. I didn't know we could do stuff like this."

Grammy laughs to herself. "And I didn't know he had such a big crush on you."

I shoot her a mortified look—both cheeks blushing bright—and she stops laughing.

"Can you make him some kind of tea or something? Reverse the spell?"

"No," Grammy answers. "Better to let this run its course. It should only last for thirty minutes or so. I wouldn't try reversing it. If you overdose him, he could forget who you are."

My eyes widen. "Has that happened before?"

She shrugs. "Let's just say there are some cousins who were better forgotten."

I smack her on the arm without thinking. "That's awful."

"So were they," she replies with a grin.

Jeffrey turns back to us. "No one's going to watch with me?"

"Celia will," Grammy volunteers. "She loves watching new shows."

"Really?" His whole face lights up. "Me too! Just one more thing to like about you . . ."

Grammy's eyes twinkle a little. I want to change my name, move to a new country, and start a new life. This might be the single most embarrassing moment . . .

". . . but there's a lot to like about you," Jeffrey is saying, his eyes back on the television. "The way you scrunch your nose when you think really hard about things. The way you're funny without being mean. Most people I know have to be mean to be funny, you know? And your smiles. The way you laugh. One time, you touched my hand and I got goose bumps."

He looks back at us, and now his cheeks are bright red.

"Just to name a few."

"Let's watch the show!" I half shout. "Let's talk about the show."

I can hear Grammy failing to stifle laughter as I walk into the living room, hoping desperately that a new focus will stop Jeffrey from announcing even more embarrassing things about me. I take the cushion on the opposite end of the couch, folding my legs beneath me. Jeffrey's already started an episode. I sit there and try to pretend that my entire world hasn't started spinning in circles.

I never let myself really believe that he liked me. I'm not sure what I thought was happening. But the words he just spoke . . . It's very, very clear how he feels about me. Jeffrey has noticed things about me that I thought only Mom and Grammy really noticed.

He actually *likes* me.

It has me feeling slightly guilty, too. The only reason he just told me all that was because we accidentally used a spell on him. There's zero chance he'd say that stuff normally. I make an effort not to ask him any more questions. Grammy's in the kitchen, and she respects the quiet that's descended over the room. We watch an episode of a show I'd probably never choose, but actually end up liking a lot. Halfway through it, Jeffrey looks over at me.

"Do you like me?"

I answer without thinking. "Yeah, I do."

He nods once, like he knew it all along, and returns his attention to the show. It's pretty clear the spell is still working. Thankfully, after about thirty minutes, Grammy intervenes.

"I'm heading out to a water aerobics class," she says. "I'm afraid Celia can't be alone at home with a friend without an adult present. It was so very nice to meet you."

Jeffrey pauses the episode, understanding immediately. He starts toward the door, pausing briefly as he passes where I'm sitting. He surprises me by leaning in for a half hug. There's a panicked swirl of thoughts as I try to remember how thoroughly I showered and what to do with my hands and all that. But it's kind of nice. A quick hug. The smell of grass on his hoodie. He slides away with another smile. Then he surprises Grammy with a hug.

"It's so nice to meet you. I've figured it all out. You're Celia's favorite."

She smiles at his bewitched honesty. As she lets him out the door, I sink back into the couch cushions, a mixture of dread and relief pounding in my chest. A hundred different truths are fighting for my attention. He likes me. He *actually* likes me. It's kind of nice, until it tangles with the second truth I've known the whole time: Jeffrey is doomed.

Not just because death has marked him, but because

this time I didn't even see the vision. I have no plan—no way to make a plan. Grammy returns to my side with a smile on her face.

"It's not funny, Grammy."

She shakes her head. "It was a *little* funny."

A laugh slips out. "A little, but . . . wow. He won't remember any of that, will he?"

Grammy shakes her head again. "I suspect not."

"So . . . was he telling the truth? Or just saying what I wanted him to say?"

"Oh please," Grammy replies. "Don't bring that self-doubt into my house, dear. He was just being more honest than normal. Doesn't mean that he didn't mean it."

The giddy feeling in my chest doesn't last long. Reality looms overhead like a dark cloud. Death is not done with Jeffrey. It might not *ever* be done. Grammy sees the look on my face and puts an arm around my shoulders. She runs her fingers through my hair like she knows exactly what I'm going to say next. It doesn't make the words any easier.

"I don't know how to save him."

CHAPTER TWENTY-THREE

A Boy's Wardrobe

All I know is that Jeffrey will wear a red hoodie on the day that he dies.

It's my one clue.

On Monday, Jeffrey wears a Lake Street Dive T-shirt. His parents bought it for him at a concert. He actually loves the band's music, and makes me listen to them one day on the bus. I can't help thinking they're the kind of music that old people like. Which makes me like Jeffrey a little more.

On Tuesday, he wears his *other* soccer hoodie. It's a divine shade of blue. Really, any color other than red is divine at this point. The hoodie seems to be Jeffrey's fashion go-to. I'm paying closer attention now, and I've figured out he's number five. When I ask, he explains it's a number that defenders usually wear. He proudly points out that on his team, he's the last line of defense, not knowing that I'm his.

On Wednesday, he wears his soccer hoodie. Again. I find myself secretly hoping that he's at least wearing a different undershirt? I don't say anything, though, because honestly, if he wore the blue hoodie every day for the rest of his life, maybe that would mean he'd live forever.

On Thursday, a button-down with a tie. Mom would say he cleans up nicely. The soccer players have to dress up on game days. I can't help thinking he looks really handsome. It'd be way, way too awkward to say that. So I just tell him that I like his tie. He keeps adjusting the knot afterward, and for the rest of the day he walks around a little more confidently.

On Friday, he wears a blue T-shirt with a dinosaur printed on it. I make fun of the design until he reveals his little brother forced him to get a matching shirt one day at

OnlyMart. He shrugs like it's no big deal, like it's not the cutest thing in the world.

And then the weekend arrives.

I have never dreaded a weekend more. School is safe. The hours are predictable. I know where Jeffrey will be for the entire day. Unless his parents grab him for a dental appointment, he's going to be safe and sound in classes I've memorized. But the weekend?

The weekend is a wild card.

A fresh wave of nervousness has me up bright and early. Grammy still beats me into the kitchen, and Mom isn't far behind. We sit in our comfortable silence around the table. Mom's reading the newspaper. Grammy's knitting something. I stare at my phone, hoping for a text. I sent one to Jeffrey right when I woke up.

It reads simply: What you up to today?

No answer so far. Not knowing is brutal. It kind of feels like there's a miniature squirrel bouncing around the walls of my stomach. I'm so distracted that my cereal has gone soggy. Mom mentions something about going out to dinner. I half listen as she lists off a few restaurants.

"Those sound good," I say.

Crossing the room, I take a seat on the couch.

My phone finally buzzes.

A text from Sophie: Still on for painting protest stuff? 11?

There's a brief moment of annoyance mixed with guilt. I forgot we planned to do that today. It's the second time I forgot about it, though. I'm staring at the text, chewing on my lip, wondering if it's a mistake to go. What if Jeffrey needs me today?

I'll have to drop everything and get to him as soon as possible. That thought connects like a lightning strike to another thought. Instead of answering Sophie, I text one of the newest numbers in my phone: Tatyana, are you available today?

The response appears instantly. I'm amazed how fast she can type, until I realize the reply is automated: I am currently with a customer. The expected wait time is: 3 minutes. JoyRide appreciates your patience. Our services will be available until 10pm tonight. Thank you for understanding.

After reading that, I decide to text Sophie back and confirm. Jeffrey's safety is a priority, but friends and family are still important too. I promised Sophie I'd come over, and I haven't exactly made a huge effort to spend time with her recently.

It's nice to have Tatyana's driving service available. If I really need to duck out and save Jeffrey, all it would take is a phone call. And hanging out with Sophie provides the perfect cover. Her parents are pretty easygoing. If I had to leave, Mom would never find out about it.

"Hey, Mom? Can you drop me off at Sophie's house? We're making protest signs."

Mom glances over. "What are you protesting?"

"Our field trip."

That catches Mom's attention.

"Wait? You're not going? I thought I signed the papers already?"

"Oh, we're totally going," I explain. "It's just a protest against the school's dress code for the event. They handed out school T-shirts that we're supposed to wear, so teachers know who's with the school and who isn't. The PTA made them white, though. For a water park. The principal decided to change the dress code for the girls. We're all supposed to wear undershirts, too. But the boys weren't given any extra requirements. Sophie said that it's . . ." I frown, trying to remember her exact words. "'Classic patriarchy shenanigans.'"

Mom nods. "I do like that Sophie. Sure! You'll be done before dinner?"

"Sometime later in the afternoon, yeah."

I feel a *little* guilty about that answer. It won't take more than an hour to paint a few signs, but I want to leave wiggle room in the schedule just in case. It'll be a lot easier to pull off a rescue that way. Mom turns the page of her newspaper. "That's fine. Go get ready."

My eyes flick from her to Grammy. I'm half expecting her to be watching me closely. She always has a knack for knowing when I'm up to something I shouldn't be doing. But her brows are furrowed as she undoes a bad stitch. I watch her a second longer, but she remains focused on her work.

Upstairs, as I'm getting ready, another text buzzes through.

It's Jeffrey.

Soccer games. Doubleheader in Kernersville. I'll be there all day.

Not good. Kernersville is *not* close. It would be expensive to ask Tatyana to take me that far. I'm actually not sure I have enough birthday money left to make it. Not to mention it'd be impossible to explain. She'd definitely have questions. And it'd be even harder to explain to Jeffrey why I was there. It's not like I can pretend I was passing through Kernersville.

I realize there's a simple solution.

After getting ready, I bound downstairs. I pose beside Grammy, and right as she looks up, I snap a selfie of the two of us. Normally, I'd never send a picture of myself to anyone. But it's the only way to make this plan work. As Grammy resumes her knitting, I type my reply.

You're missing a big day in the Cleary household

I send it with the picture of the two of us.

Jeffrey sends back three laughing emojis. *Come on*, I think, *take the bait*. My phone is quiet for a long and painful minute. And then it buzzes. A picture comes through.

It's an image of him sitting in the front seat of a car. His little brother is strapped in a seat behind him. He's angled the picture so that it looks like he's about to eat his brother, who's laughing hysterically. But the best part? The best part is that he's wearing his blue hoodie.

Relief floods through me. I plunk down in the chair next to Grammy and feel twenty pounds lighter. He's going to live today. I don't have to rush off to some random town.

I'm typing in a response when Grammy appears at my shoulder. She glances down at my phone and makes a scandalized face.

"Celia! You're posting photos of me to the internet? I'm in my nightwear!"

Mom appears, keys in hand. "Ready, Celia?"

"Ready!" I confirm, grinning at Grammy. "You look fine!"

She huffs. "Fine? I do not look *fine*. Can you recall it?"

I laugh again. "It's just a text, Grammy."

She shakes her head. "I've got a few photos of *you* I could text. . . ."

Mom intervenes. "No social media, Gram. You remember what happened last time. With the neighborhood's Facebook page?"

Grammy shrugs innocently. "I'm not sure what you're talking about."

Mom raises an eyebrow as she opens the door.

"Gram. You told people the pool was closed *before* it closed."

Grammy nods, finally remembering. "Ah yes. The rare scatological prophecy."

Mom makes a disgusted noise. "Exactly. No social media."

Grammy looks chastised, but throws me a wink the second Mom is out of sight. I can't help laughing. Mom must have forgotten the time Grammy told everyone that the Girl Scout cookies were going to make them sick. There were several angry troop leaders, until people actually started having stomach issues. All that attention made Grammy realize it wasn't a good idea to have her prophecies time-stamped.

I leave the house with Mom, feeling the freedom of a *weekend* for the first time in months. Sophie's house is about fifteen minutes away. I can tell Mom's in a good mood just based on the music station she chooses. She hums along to the first song before looking over at me.

"So, how's the whole prophecy thing going?"

Her question lands on my head like a brick. I take a second to steady myself before answering. Grammy coached me through this a while ago. Be honest, but not too honest.

"It's hard."

Mom nods. "New things are always hard. But you like it?"

That question catches me off guard too. It's been about a month now. I've been so *busy* that I've almost forgotten that what I'm doing is *actually* magic. Without the visions, Jeffrey would have died. A car accident. A tragic story in the paper. A funeral our classmates might have attended. I haven't exactly won the fight against death yet, but what I've done so far has made a difference.

"I do like it," I say. "I really do."

Mom nods again. "I know I can't fully—understand. Gram didn't teach me much about it, really. Guess she didn't see the point. But I grew up knowing how different she was.

The way she just could *sense* things. About me and about other people. So I might not get how it all works, but I do want you to know that it's not like I'm against the magic. I'm really . . . proud of you."

Until now, I'd kind of thought she didn't like it.

"Thanks, Mom."

She smiles at me. "It helped talking with your aunt. The things Mary and Martha can do? They're such brilliant girls. And your Grammy is an example of using her gifts to do good. I just didn't want you to fall into the trap her sister did. You know about Susan?"

I nod. "She lives in Texas."

"She's *barricaded* in Texas," Mom corrects. "The visions were too much for her. She found them overwhelming. She doesn't really have any contact with the outside world now. Your grandmother told me she sees too many possibilities. Whatever that means."

Her fear makes more sense than ever. I've always known this was a part of her hesitation. If you don't know how the gifts work, all you can see is the *result* of the magic. There are examples of both good and bad outcomes in our family. And now that I've started, I understand better than ever. Saving Jeffrey over and over, I could totally see someone snapping under that pressure.

"I'm not sure I'm saying it the right way," Mom continues. "What I really wanted to say is that I hope you're doing the best you can with what you're given. That's the only thing I've ever really believed was important. Whether your talent is math, or prophecies, or the guitar. I don't really care one bit what you want to do. I just hope you're doing the best you can with what you have."

She pulls into Sophie's neighborhood.

"How do you know?"

Mom lifts an eyebrow. "Know what?"

"That you're doing your best? Or that you're making the best choice?"

"I think you just feel it." She taps her chest. "In here."

Her answer echoes how I've felt this whole time. Even as Grammy warned and cautioned, I've always *felt* deep down that I'm making the right decision. People are worth saving.

Jeffrey is worth saving. He was at the start. Even more so now that I've gotten to know who he is.

"Thanks, Mom."

She smiles again as we pull into Sophie's driveway. I lean across and give her a quick kiss on the cheek. "I'll call you when we're done."

"Love you, honey."

I wave as she backs out of the driveway. I feel lighter than I have in weeks. One day of knowing Jeffrey is safe. One day of knowing my mom isn't mad about my prophecies, that I don't have to tiptoe around her like I thought I did. One day of hanging out with friends and being normal. The sun shines overhead, and it's like it's shining just for me.

CHAPTER TWENTY-FOUR

The Final Piece of the Puzzle

Sophie and I get to work immediately. I'm a little surprised that we're not using signs this time. She brings out a bunch of T-shirts instead. This protest has been planned for weeks now. Her message is a wake-up call to the administration. Boys and girls have to be treated equally.

It's a worthy cause, but when Sophie shows me her first attempt, I see the main reason that she invited me over. "Is that supposed to be a W? Or an X?"

Sophie frowns. "I'm really not sure."

I'm still squinting at the word. "Hard to get your point across if no one can read it."

"I know," Sophie replies. "That's why you're here."

She sifts through an OnlyMart bag, setting out two more blank T-shirts. Both are the same ugly shade of maroon. I hold the shirt up to the light, and it actually looks like dragon's blood or something. "Interesting color choice."

"They were out of blue," Sophie replies. "It's not that bad."

I smile. "Okay. Hand me the paintbrush."

We take a few minutes to figure out the best slogans before getting to work. Sophie sings my praises the whole time. It's definitely not perfect, but my versions are at least legible. We make several different shirts before setting them out to dry. Without thinking, I send a picture to Jeffrey of our progress. He and DeSean are the only other ones who really know about the protest.

I follow Sophie into the backyard. It's huge compared to ours. All enclosed by a fence. There's a random camping tent set up in the middle. We walk past it, aiming for hammocks they have in the back corner. "Why do you have a tent out here?"

Sophie shrugs. "We camped outside a couple nights ago."

"Really?"

"Yeah. Dad likes sleeping under the stars. Mom always says we protest so that everyone has the same chance to live a good life, but that being a good protester *also* means enjoying the life you're protesting for. I forget that part sometimes. They always try to remind me."

We pick separate hammocks. It's nice to swing in the half-hearted sunlight. For a few minutes, it's just the breeze and the sound of our bodies swaying.

"I'm glad you didn't ditch us," Sophie says.

I remember what she asked the other day, about me "pulling an Avery."

"Why would I ever ditch you?"

"The same reason Avery did," Sophie says. "Jeffrey's one of the cool kids."

That thought almost makes me laugh. "Is he?"

"You know what I mean. He's a soccer player. And he's hot."

A blush creeps over my cheeks. Sophie's always been blunt. It's not that I don't think Jeffrey is "hot," but I'd never actually say that out loud. Sophie sees my expression and rolls her eyes.

"Oh, pull it together, Cleary."

I laugh. I've always loved that she calls me "Cleary." It's different than Jeffrey's version of the nickname, though. Sophie uses it like a drill sergeant. Jeffrey makes the name into an inside joke, like he's referring to a version of me that only he knows about.

"You're the one that said he's hot," I point out.

Sophie smiles. "Just speaking the truth."

I think back to what Mary said about letting other people in. Sophie's been my friend for a few years now. If I can't trust her, who can I trust? Still, it's a struggle to find the right words.

"I've been distracted, but it's not Jeffrey's fault. Well, not technically. You know about my grandmother's business, right?"

Sophie frowns. "The psychic thing?"

My stomach knots up a little. "Yeah. The psychic thing. It's what she does. It's what she's done her whole life. And I've always kind of . . . known that I would do it too. If that makes sense?"

That draws Sophie's attention. "Really?"

I'm surprised by the tone of her voice. It's not *really*, as in *You seriously think that's real?* It's more of a curious *really*. It gives me a boost in confidence.

"Yeah. Our family is kind of weird. We have a . . . *sense* of things. It's hard to explain, I guess. But it starts on our 4,444th day."

Sophie is staring at me now. "That's oddly specific."

I smile. "I know. That's a big part of why I've been distracted. It's not just Jeffrey. There's this whole other . . . thing. I've been struggling in school. It's been a tough month. So . . . I'm sorry. I didn't mean to be a distracted friend."

Sophie's eyes drift up to the sky. Her voice is full of relief.

"I'm so glad you're weird like me."

I laugh at that. It comes bubbling out of me because, honestly, I thought she'd respond the same way that Avery did.

The idea that she'd just accept me as I am is kind of startling.

"Thanks, Sophie." I sigh. "And with Jeffrey . . . I do like him. I just don't want to mess anything up. Lunches have been fun. We've got a good group."

Sophie nods, more serious now. "That's why I didn't go on a date with DeSean."

Another jolt runs through my system. I sit up so fast that my hammock threatens to flip.

"DeSean?"

"Yeah. He's the one who sits with us at lunch," Sophie jokes, like I've forgotten who he is. "Really funny kid? Has a famous Instagram account only we know about?"

"I *know* who DeSean is! But what do you mean? Did he ask you out?"

"A while ago." Sophie nods. "I told him if I wanted to date, I would ask *him* out."

Now I'm laughing. "Of course. What did he say?"

"He made a PowerPoint presentation," Sophie says, unable to keep the laughter out of her voice now. "Of all the reasons I should reconsider."

We're both laughing, our hammocks shaking, because of course DeSean made a presentation. He's always been super organized. We always fought over who got to be his project partner, because we knew it was a guaranteed A+.

"And?"

Sophie shrugs. "It had nice sound effects."

I double over again.

"Sophie, come on. You know what I mean. It's DeSean. We love DeSean."

"DeSean is great," Sophie says. "But I have a lot I want to do. I need to stay focused. I wasn't trying to hurt his feelings or anything. If I want a boyfriend, I'll ask him out on a date. That's that."

We both hang there, smiling at the sky, until Sophie throws another lightning bolt of a question in my direction. "Are you going to date Jeffrey?"

There's no way to sink lower into the hammock, but my body tries to anyways.

"I don't know."

"Just promise me," Sophie says, "that you'll ask *him* out.

That's why we made the shirts. Equality. I don't want you waiting around for him to buy you popcorn or something."

I smile at her. "Promise. Although, popcorn sounds kind of good right now . . ."

Another breeze sets the leaves above us to trembling. The sun politely sneaks through gaps in the trees, warming our skin. I'm enjoying the calm—knowing Jeffrey is safe, at least for today—when a missing piece in the puzzle clicks into place.

The text I sent Jeffrey. It feels like déjà vu.

That's not something that *exists* for seers. There's no such thing as déjà vu in Grammy's world. If something happens again, if a phrase is spoken twice in one day, there's something crucially important about it. I sit up enough to see our painted shirts hanging from the nearby railing. It takes my brain a second to process the fact that they're *red*.

An ugly red. More like maroon. Different enough that I didn't notice the connection at first, but the hoodie Jeffrey's supposed to die in next is *also* red. And his shirt had something painted on the front. A detail my brain struggled to remember in the moments after the vision. Seeing the hand-painted letters on our own shirts, however, brings that detail back bright and bold in my mind. I can see the words:

THE FEMPIRE STRIKES BACK.

That was what was written on Jeffrey's shirt. Not *just* a *Star Wars* reference. Clearly, those words are connected to the protest. And they weren't printed on his shirt either. The letters were hand-drawn. In Jeffrey's handwriting.

"I'm the one who caused . . ."

Sophie stirs enough to get a look at me. "What?"

I shake my head. "Nothing."

I'm certain now. Jeffrey will make his own protest shirt. I have no idea if he's seen my text or not yet, but it's impossible for someone like me to *not* see what happens next. I've become a piece on the game board of death and fate. He'll see our red shirts. He'll see the hand-painted messages. And he will paint his own protest on an old hoodie.

A red one.

Which means his death is the day of the field trip.

I lie there, quietly considering the options. It would be so easy to text him. I could say that the shirts didn't look good, so we threw them away. It would stop him from making a hoodie, but would that be enough to stop his death? I grind my teeth in frustration.

Instead of texting him, I slide my phone back into a pocket. It's better this way. Now I know he's supposed to die on the field trip. At Jungle Rapids. Grammy always told me that knowledge is power. Knowing these details means I can make a plan.

I can save him.

CHAPTER TWENTY-FIVE

Making a Plan

Mom taught me the importance of preparation.

I was her official quiz-giver before big cases. I'd snuggle up in her bed, surrounded by a sea of color-coded index cards. She'd have me read them, one by one, as she paced the room. Each one had a random detail from her research. I'd read it and she'd dive into that part of the case by memory. It was a fun game she always won. One time, I asked what the point of practicing was if she already knew it all.

Life is unpredictable, but the more you know, the less likely you are to be surprised.

Ironic advice from the daughter of a seer. But this time, it's her advice I need more than Grammy's. I don't know what's going to happen. I don't have a vision of how Jeffrey will die. So I prepare for Tuesday's field trip, and I'm glad that I'm my mother's daughter. She trained me well. Fill in the gaps. Study the details. Win the case.

Step one: research Jungle Rapids.

I got to go four or five years ago, but the park has changed. I'm thankful that there's a detailed breakdown of each attraction on their official website. Maps and videos and more. I print out a copy of the park's map before going through each section. I do my best to mark the areas that feel the most dangerous. Which is the problem: literally everything is dangerous.

There's the Go-Kart track. Hairpin turns sectioned off by shamefully low walls. The vehicles have "governors" installed that will reduce their speed, but it still feels like Jeffrey is just one wrong turn, one broken part away, from disaster.

At first glance, the Laser Tag zone feels safe, but I pull up one of the commercial videos. It shows kids moving stealthily through a huge area that has an upper story. There are safety barriers on the second level, and a no-running policy, but there's no way any of Jeffrey's soccer teammates would ever obey that rule. I highlight the entire upper floor as a potential threat.

My eyes trace over the section about the Rock Wall. I highlight all of it.

Great.

The Jungle Golf zone looks safe enough. And so does the Arcade. I look around at the layouts and can't help thinking that if I can keep Jeffrey in those areas, there's a chance I'll actually keep him alive. But then I stumble upon the most dangerous area in the whole park. And the area Jeffrey's most likely to want to go: the Water Park.

I can feel my heart rate rising as I click through the pictures. There are three waterslides. One brags that it is the longest and fastest in the state. I cluck my tongue like a grandmother. There's one section called the MegaWinder, and it looks the kind of thing that could fling a middle-schooler into space. "Why do these even *exist*?" I whisper to myself.

Last but not least, the Lazy River and the Wave Pool. Each one comes with varying degrees of danger. I know the Lazy River is supposed to be a calm place, but the last time I visited, my cousins spent half the time boarding each other's tubes as they floated downstream. And I'm not sure I've ever entered a Wave Pool without *feeling* like I was close to dying. There's always a swarm of people, and all it takes is one wrong move to end up pinned to a wall, the waves crashing overhead.

I memorize the locations of every lifeguard stand. It feels like slapping a Band-Aid on a gaping wound, though. The reality is that Jeffrey could end up in any area I've marked. Which means I need to be with him the whole time.

That brings me to step two.

After Grammy goes to bed, I head downstairs. The Cleary Family Guide Book sits on the shelf, where it usually is. I smuggle the guide back to my room. About two hours later, I finally find the right potion. It's not connected to my magical specialization, so there's no real way of knowing if I can actually use it or not, but this might be my best bet. I write down the ingredients in a notebook before turning my attention to step three.

Monday arrives. It is a day full of distractions.

Teachers have us reading out loud. There are articles and poems and geometrical shapes. I know there's writing on the board, but nothing really makes it to my brain. Most of our school is buzzing with excitement. Tomorrow is the big day. Our first field trip of the year.

In the last class of the day, I ask to use the bathroom. Sitting in one of the back stalls, I send a text to Tatyana: Can I get a 2:50 pickup in the Green?

I'm not sure if she's in class or not, but my phone buzzes ten seconds later.

I'll be there.

Earlier, I considered having her pick me up at school to save time. But that would mean not taking the bus home with Jeffrey. He sits across from me today and talks about his soccer games. There's a secret hiding in his smile, and as we leave the bus, he says, "I've got a surprise for you."

I already know what it is, but I smile anyway. "Oh yeah? Let's see it."

"Tomorrow," he promises. "Pretty sure you're gonna like it."

And that little glimpse of him almost breaks me into pieces. My mind wrestles with all of it. We always think the next day is coming. Sometimes, today is so boring—so *normal*—that we don't even think of how lucky we are to have tomorrow. Jeffrey thinks tomorrow will be a field trip. Another normal day. He has no idea he was supposed to die almost a month ago.

I push all those feelings aside. I have to stay focused.

He walks with me, and our hands keep bouncing into each other. It takes a second to realize he's kind of intentionally putting his hand that close to mine. I can feel the heat creeping up my neck. I pretend to dig through one pocket for something, but I'm really just making sure my palms aren't sweaty. Jeffrey looks ridiculously nervous now, so I reach out and take his hand.

He almost jumps. His eyes dart over to me. He closes his hand around mine, and for the first few seconds it's like two crabs trying to hold claws. We're so awkward and this is so new that none of it feels right. Until his fingers interlock with mine.

And even though his palm is a little sweaty, it's kind of the best feeling in the world. We walk down to the corner like that and I find myself looking around, nervous someone else is watching or laughing. But it's just the two of us, and the sun shining overhead. He smiles a goodbye.

I watch as he walks down his street. It's hard to tell for sure, but he almost looks like he's inspecting his hand and trying to figure out if it's still functional or not. Instead of heading home, I turn back around. Grammy's probably there. I know Mom isn't. I have just enough time for the next step in the plan.

I double back to the Green. A man walks past with his dog. Tatyana arrives exactly one minute before our scheduled time. Her engine fires and rumbles.

She pulls into the same spot where I met her last time. I jump into the back of the car and nod. She speaks first.

"Where are we heading today? Another lunch *date*?"

I'm not sure why I thought she'd forget. I asked her to take me to a random restaurant, and then I saved the life of a boy who clearly wasn't there to meet me. Tatyana is looking at me in the rearview mirror. Her expression is a reminder: she knows *something* is up.

"I just want to go to Starbucks."

Her eyes narrow. "There are like seven of them. Which location?"

"How about the one in Regency?"

She pulls up the address. Her engine thunders. The man with the dog looks up, like he wants to tell us to slow down, but Tatyana's around the corner before he can say a word. I settle into the seat, trying to avoid eye contact, but Tatyana's curiosity can't be avoided.

"Never got to ask you about that day," she says. When I don't speak, she probes again. "Pretty cool. You saving him like that. It was pretty cool."

I have no idea what she suspects, but I nod. "It was pretty lucky."

She doesn't push the conversation as we pull into the Starbucks parking lot.

"I'll be right back."

There's a short line. A few kids from the high school, but no one I know. I order a drink that I don't plan on drinking, and then I ask for two extra cups with two extra lids. The barista shrugs before retrieving everything. I shove the extras into my book bag, wait for my drink, and leave.

Tatyana looks disappointed. "No secret rendezvous this time?"

"I just wanted some coffee. Can you drop me back off in the Green?"

The drive home is somehow shorter. It's almost magical, the way she knows every shortcut and somehow catches every light. I decide not to mention concepts of magic, in case she starts asking questions again. She eases back into the same parking spot about eight minutes later. Before I can open the door, she catches my eye in the mirror.

"You know, I was thinking about the other day," she says.

"At the Crab Shack. He got in the car after you saved him. And he had no idea you were going to be there. Did he?"

I swallow, but don't say anything.

"I thought so," she continues. "Don't worry. I won't make you explain it. And I won't tell anyone. I'm running a business here. I'm a professional. I just wanted to make sure I wasn't losing my mind. Not sure how you knew, but I'm glad you saved him. DeSean hangs out with Jeffrey now. He's a good kid."

The awkwardness stretches until I hold out a ten-dollar bill.

"Thanks for the ride."

"This one's on me. Be careful out there, okay?"

I'm surprised by her generosity. I pocket the money and start heading home. I can feel the two cups pressing through the material of my backpack. It's time for step four: the actual magic.

Grammy's home. She smiles up from the kitchen table and asks about my day, and I do my best to act the way I'm *supposed* to act. Stressed about Jeffrey's potential death.

Annoyed that homework still exists. I sit at the table, and she offers little nibbles of advice.

Mom comes home in time for a late dinner. We catch a few episodes of *Vampire High*. When Grammy starts snoozing in her chair, Mom nudges her and suggests going to bed. She smiles a good night to us. The exact second her door closes, I'm in the kitchen.

Earlier, when I tried to take a picture of the spell book, it kept coming out fuzzy. I raised an eyebrow at that, but quickly realized the magic of the book didn't *allow* the information to be copied. Kind of cool. Also a little inconvenient. It means I have to use the actual book. I turn to the right page, trying not to catch Mom's eye, and run back through the ingredients.

There's a big blue pot that Grammy uses for soups sometimes. It's perfect for the potion. I set it out on the counter and start working my way through the recipe.

Pour in water. Light a bayberry candle. Hold mint leaves over the flame until singed. Add those to the water. Follow with ginseng shavings. Stir thrice, always clockwise. Add a good measure of honey (more for taste than effect). The final direction suggests thinking a kind thought before closing the lid. I shut my eyes, imagining Jeffrey alive and well, before securing the potion inside. I can't help smiling.

This is the second potion I've brewed. I'm starting to feel like a proper witch.

Mom's still watching TV as I position the pot in the back corner of the fridge, using a carton of yogurt to hide as much of it as I can. All that's left to do now is boil it in the morning. And then we move to step five, which is the one step I'm getting used to executing at this point.

Save Jeffrey Johnson.

CHAPTER TWENTY-SIX

Welcome to Jungle Rapids!

Tuesday morning arrives.

I get dressed and it feels like preparation for battle. Downstairs, I'm braced for the first likely obstacle: Grammy. She has a knack for knowing when something *big* is about to happen. The perks of being a seer, I guess. As I come down this morning, however, the kitchen is empty.

No words of warning are scrawled on the notepad attached to the fridge. I stand by the table, listening. Mom is in the shower. Grammy's room is silent. I'm surprised to find the TV still on with a promotional image for *Vampire High* glowing on our wide-screen. Mom's always pretty obsessed about turning it off to save energy or whatever. I do my best to ignore the distraction. This is my best chance.

I dart over to the fridge, shoving aside containers, and carefully remove the massive blue pot. Liquid sloshes within. It takes less than five minutes to get the potion up to a boil. Mom's shower goes quiet. There's no sign of Grammy still.

The spell advises not to let the liquid get *too* hot. Boiling away the ingredients weakens the magic. It also suggests not letting the tea cool, which can have adverse effects.

Enter Starbucks.

I remove the two borrowed cups. The liquid is churning nicely. Carefully I use a ladle to scoop equal amounts into both. As I do, the first unexpected problem arrives.

"No way . . ."

There's not quite enough. I'm not sure if the boiling reduced the mixture, or if I just messed up the measurements? The liquid fills each cup to the halfway mark. It doesn't ruin my plan, but I was definitely hoping to make the spell last all day. Now there's a chance it runs out.

I briefly consider adding more water, but I think there was a note in the margins advising against that. Sighing, I tighten the lids. I'll just have to improvise at the park.

A door opens. I set the bewitched teas off to one side as Mom enters.

"Good morning," she says. "I dreamed about vampires last night."

I smile, using the distracted moment to lower the blue pot into the dirty side of the sink. "Watching too much TV," I say in my most motherly voice. "It'll rot your brain."

She smiles back and heads straight for the coffeepot. "Grammy?"

"Haven't seen her yet."

Mom frowns, turning. "Well, there's your answer. I turned the TV off last night. She must have woken up and come out to watch what she missed. Bet she stayed up *way* too late."

I smile. "Funny how she pretends not to like the show."

"More like stubborn," Mom replies before pointing to my shirt. "So the field trip is today? I like the shirt."

The message reads:

WITHOUT ANNABETH, PERCY WOULD

HAVE DIED.

"If you like mine, you'd love Sophie's."

"You're a good kid," Mom says in approval. "Don't miss the bus, or the only person reading that will be a substitute teacher."

There's zero chance I'll get a better invitation to leave than that. Quietly I gather my things. I can't help glancing at Grammy's room. There's a familiar battle raging inside me. A natural desire to talk through my plan with her. I want to show off the magic *she* taught me to love. But the other half knows sneaking out the door right now will keep her from interfering. I know this is my best shot at saving Jeffrey. So I cradle both teas, kiss Mom's cheek, and leave.

I'm halfway up the road, absently humming the song Grammy always does, when Jeffrey comes into sight. The other kids from our neighborhood are gathered at the bus stop, but the grin on Jeffrey's face makes them all look like shadows. He stands proudly in his red hoodie. The surprise he promised is painted across his chest: THE FEMPIRE STRIKES BACK. Those words bring the image of my vision echoing into reality.

It's a confirmation. Today is the day Jeffrey is supposed to die.

He stretches the material for my inspection. "Like it?"

"Very cool of you," I reply with a smile. "Sophie will appreciate the *Star Wars* reference too."

I'm doing my best to focus on Jeffrey's slightly crooked smile, the hand-lettering on his hoodie. But as the doors open and everyone scrambles onto the bus, all I can see is what *surrounds* Jeffrey. It tugs on me like a sixth sense. Dark threads appear briefly in my vision, lurking overhead. Death is here. It's in the air.

I smile because I want death to know I'm not afraid. I hand Jeffrey one of the teas.

"Got this for you."

He doesn't even ask what it is. Just takes that first sip.

"Nice!"

On the bus, I can't help noticing Avery *noticing* us. She throws a few glances back as Jeffrey and I sip our matching teas. I know she's still upset from the breakup with Jordan Lyles. Any other day, I'd consider saying something, but I don't have time for distractions. Not today.

I have no idea how long it will take for the magic to kick in, so I encourage Jeffrey to drink the whole thing. The face he makes is priceless. "It's very . . . uhh . . . grassy."

Which is a very polite way to put it. I'm fighting through a bitter aftertaste that's only getting worse as I get to the bottom. I'm thankful that Jeffrey doesn't make me guilt him into finishing the drink. He tilts his head back, shakes his head, and smiles.

"Thanks for grabbing me a drink."

After a few minutes, I feel a sensation.

It's like an invisible thread. Almost as if someone's looping a painless needle down the left side of my body. The thread tightens and loosens, tightens and loosens. And then one thought pulses in my mind. It's like a little voice making a very polite but important suggestion.

I should hang out with Jeffrey today.

He looks at me like he just had the same exact thought. In the back of my mind, I fight to remember what's happening. I used a binding spell. The magic will keep both of us together today. Jeffrey leans a little closer to me. Even if it's the magic, I still feel incredibly awkward, like everyone is watching us.

The magic whispers in my ear: *Don't worry about that. Today is about the both of you.*

Jeffrey blurts out, "What do you want to do first? At the park?"

I almost say *Be with you*, but I am a seer. I will not be bossed around by my own magic. I bury that first thought and settle my mind. Jeffrey's waiting.

I shrug. "I'd love to start with Putt-Putt."

The other day, he was raving to DeSean about the slides, but hearing my suggestion, he nods like I've just come up with the best idea in the world. The bus stops a minute later. We all file out. The other grade levels head to their assigned meet-up areas, all excited for the big field trip.

Jeffrey's shoulder is pretty much pinned against mine. Or did I pin mine against his?

The spell is still weaving us magically together. I can't help smiling. It works. My potion actually works. We join a rowdy herd of seventh graders outside the entrance to the cafeteria. Inside, it's easy to spot Sophie. She's standing up on a table. Her bright red shirt reads:

KEEP YOUR POLICIES OFF MY BODY

Massive piles of T-shirts are stacked on the built-in seats in front of her. I knew her mom had been receiving donations for the last few weeks, but never guessed they'd gotten so many. There are literally hundreds of them, separated and labeled by size.

I can't tell if it's Jeffrey's idea to head toward her or mine, but we walk in step like some kind of choreographed dance team. Sophie is listening to an ongoing conversation between Mrs. Honea and Principal Locklear. Locklear stands there for a few seconds before shrugging once and giving Sophie a thumbs-up. My eyes widen as he starts walking to the microphone on the run-down stage.

"What happened, Sophie?"

She raises one fist. "Equality is happening, Cleary. Equality."

That awful microphone sound slashes through the air. Everyone winces a little before Locklear pulls the microphone up and away. "Quick announcement. Before you separate into classes for loading onto the bus, we'll be requiring an alteration to the dress code for boys. On the original form, we required that the girls wear an undershirt beneath their school-provided T-shirts, which are white. We will now be requiring all boys to do the same. If you do not already have an undershirt on, I'll ask that you line up at the center of the room.

"There are appropriate sizes for everyone, shirts provided by Sophie Pires." He pauses for emphasis. "It was brought to my attention that the rules of our field trip were biased. We always tell you to go out with Patriot pride! And that means being proud of how we do things in this building. Thanks for pointing this out to us, Sophie. Get to it, boys."

Sophie might as well be wearing a crown. A few boys

stumble over, and she starts directing them to the right piles. DeSean shoulders through the crowd a few seconds later.

"Did I miss it?"

"Barely," I reply. "Locklear just agreed to a new policy. Sophie wins."

In a very un-DeSean-like move, he vaults up onto the table and hugs Sophie. She smiles back at him before pointing to a pile on the right. "You can start handing out the larges!"

It's our first victory of the day, hopefully a sign of things to come.

It doesn't take long for the madness to settle back down. No one complains. Sophie is practically glowing as we pile onto the bus. The spell has solidified by now. Jeffrey and I are threaded together. In the back of my mind, I'm kind of starting to worry that I overdid the potion. What happens if I have to go to the bathroom? I hope he doesn't try to follow me inside.

I thought the spell would make it easy to keep Jeffrey from randomly running off with his soccer buddies. But right now, even I'm having trouble fighting against the magic's magnetic pull.

The ride to Jungle Rapids is mercifully short. Just thirty minutes of forced school chants and obnoxious laughter and excitement. I find myself thankful Jeffrey took a shower this morning. I have a feeling we're going to be *very* close today. My eyes trace the red hoodie that's become an emblem of death in my mind, and I have to stare out the window to not get upset.

I'm not going to lose you.

Not today.

We arrive.

A disorderly piling-off process happens. Shoulders bumping, voices echoing, and then the bright sunshine welcoming us out into a pothole-ridden parking lot. It's not too hot yet, but several students are already applying spray-on sunscreen. Chaperones circle the group, counting us like sheep. One of the assistant principals is looming at the front entrance, ordering folks around. Jeffrey stands at my side.

The spell whispers in my ear: *Where else would he go?*

Sophie is still in a celebratory mood. That's good news. I don't love the idea of manipulating anyone, but I have a feeling she'll be more willing to do the activities I suggest after her big victory. And DeSean clearly wants to do whatever she does. It's the perfect setup. I take a deep breath as the final head count happens. They start sending us in, about fifteen students at a time, so the people working the front desk won't be overwhelmed.

Over the nearest fence, I can see park attendants scrambling in preparation for three hundred chaotic students to enter. Beyond them, the waterslides stand watch, both of them higher than most of the buildings in our town. My stomach knots together nervously.

I can do this.

The line moves and our group is next.

I try to make my voice loud and confident. "Who's up for Putt-Putt?"

Mrs. Honea signals us forward. The others nod.

Overhead, a WELCOME TO JUNGLE RAPIDS! sign swallows us.

CHAPTER TWENTY-SEVEN

Trouble in River City

About an hour into the field trip, I feel like I'm winning.

Against death.

Too bad I'm losing miserably at Putt-Putt.

"Celia, I'm surprised you wanted to play a second round," DeSean notes.

Jeffrey sinks a ten-foot putt. "She's just falling behind for a more dramatic victory."

"Hey. I'm not that far behind."

Sophie holds up the scorecard. "It would take a miracle at this point."

I make a face and do my best to ignore the thought that comes to mind. *I can't waste miracles on golf. I need them all for Jeffrey.* As we move on to the last hole of our second round of Putt-Putt, I'm already plotting my next move to keep him safe.

From our slightly elevated position in the park, we have a perfect view of the Go-Kart track. Every now and again, the little vehicles come zooming past. I can see the looks of longing on Jeffrey's and DeSean's faces. Even if Jeffrey is magically glued to my side, I'm going to have a hard time convincing the rest of the group to play any more golf today.

Which means it's time to change things up. My goal is to make it safely to lunch. And that means I need to move us to the second-safest place in the park.

"We should go to the Arcade next."

All I have to do is make the suggestion. A second later, Jeffrey takes up the cause like it's the only thing he's ever wanted to do. "Time Crisis!" he shouts. "The Jump-Jeep game! I'd be down for some Immortus! Great idea, Cleary."

After Sophie putts, we all start walking downhill toward the final hole.

"I was hoping we'd hit the waterslides next," DeSean says. "Didn't you want to go on the Thundercat?"

He looks at Jeffrey, who glances over at me. When he sees my lack of interest, he shrugs back. "Eventually! Let's do the Arcade first."

I do my best to ignore the awkward silence, focusing on my putt instead. The bright blue golf ball swirls around before disappearing into the tunneled hole that's always on number eighteen. The others finish. Thankfully, DeSean doesn't say anything about Jeffrey's weird change in attitude.

Next up: the Arcade.

It ends up being a lot of fun. DeSean and Jeffrey get locked into some kind of military combat game that has them deep in enemy territory. I supply them with more quarters, trying to stretch every minute into two, but they eventually decide the final boss can't be beaten.

I'm looking around, thinking about guiding them to some new challenge, when the art teacher—Mr. Wiley—swings past. "Lunchtime! It's open to our group for the next hour. Go ahead over to the River City section of the park. Burgers, hot dogs, french fries!"

He spots another group of students and heads off to deliver the same message.

I smile to myself. The day really couldn't be going any better. There's even a small part of me that wonders if I've already won. I never saw the *actual* vision of Jeffrey's death. Without me, he might have gone to the slides first, or over to the Wave Pool. It's possible I already saved him. But there's no way to know, not until we leave the park for good.

Jeffrey's laughing at a picture that Sophie took of him and DeSean. I follow a few steps behind, my eyes scanning every doorway and rooftop, just in case random objects threaten to come spiraling from above. Nothing happens, though. We reach River City safely.

The area is sectioned off by fences that look like cresting waves. Inside, hundreds of plastic tables with backless seats await. I'm pretty sure they've been there for a few decades. Families are exiting the area as our middle school slowly takes over the place. A crew of Jeffrey's soccer buddies sits by the entrance. I notice Hunter, Tyreek, and Everett seated there. Most of them are wearing red bandannas with the team's logo printed on the front. Jeffrey bumps knuckles with Everett as we pass by.

The place is full of laughter and sunlight and hot dogs.

Our group decides to divide and conquer. DeSean and Sophie collapse at a corner table that's partially decorated with mustard. Jeffrey follows my lead to wait in line at the food hut. As we reach the front of the line, I'm thinking through strategies that will get us safely to three p.m.

A disinterested college kid rings us up. He's in a Hawaiian shirt and looks like he'd rather be anywhere else in the world. I hand him our four lunch vouchers before Jeffrey orders his food and DeSean's. I order for Sophie and then myself.

"Hot dog or cheeseburger?" the cashier asks in a bored voice.

"Burger," I reply distractedly. "No cheese."

A breeze has the flags attached to the food stand swaying. The guy finishes our order, and I look over to find Jeffrey staring at me. "What? What's wrong? Are you okay?"

For a second, I imagine death being cruel enough to kill him in some way I can't prevent. A brain aneurysm or something. But Jeffrey shakes his head, a clear sign of life.

"No cheese? Who doesn't like cheese on their burger?"

He's grinning at me as he starts heading for the condiment stand. I stand there smiling until a throat clears. The cashier is impatiently holding out two drinks.

"Your boyfriend forgot his Coke."

It's one of those moments that feels like a dream. A really *bad* dream. Why would he say that? And why would he say it so loud? I don't dare look around, but I feel like everyone in earshot is watching me now. Is that what they all think? That Jeffrey and I are together?

Without thinking, I throw back an answer. "He's not my boyfriend!"

The cashier's already looking at the next person in line, though, which means I turn in time to catch the embarrassed look on Jeffrey's face. Maybe he would have been embarrassed by what the cashier was saying, but that embarrassment is nothing compared to his reaction to what I just said. He looks like someone who's been abandoned at a train station or something. I can see the hurt written on his face at how quickly I turned down the idea of being his girlfriend.

I'm trying to figure out how to apologize when I see the one thing he doesn't. With his eyes on me and his cheeks flushing red, he doesn't notice the caution sign that's been set out. He doesn't see the puddle of soda waiting between him and the condiment table.

His feet slick forward. His arms shoot out. His whole body arches backward. It's like watching a cartoon character slip on a banana. It doesn't even look real.

My instincts take over.

I've spent the whole morning bracing for impact, ready to ward off any potential threat. So my body knows what to do. I drop the drinks I'm holding and lunge forward. My extended hands catch him beneath the shoulder blades and barely keep him from smashing his head against the concrete. He's bigger than me, though, so the weight tears across my lower back.

Momentum has me stumbling into the nearest person.

They go down with a scream.

All the noise draws attention. Pretty much everyone in River City looks our way. I'm on the ground, groaning loudly. I'm thankful to see Jeffrey roll over on his back and blink. He's alive. Relief pulses through me. Was that the moment? Did I save him?

It's only as I push up into a sitting position that I realize the other person I accidentally decked is Avery. "Oh! Sorry, Avery! Are you okay?"

She's wincing. "My ankle . . . I think . . ."

I know Avery well enough to know she'd never pretend something is worse than it is. She's always been tough. There aren't any bones punching up through skin or anything, but I can tell she's really in pain. I feel horrible. It doesn't help that she landed in the puddle created by our spilled sodas. I can see the liquid soaking through the edges of her shorts. Jeffrey pushes up to his feet as Mrs. Honea arrives.

"Oh dear. I'll get some ice," she says. "Anyone else hurt?"

Jeffrey shakes his head. "I'm fine."

I nod to her. "Same."

Avery winces again. I can tell she's looking around, trying to see if people are laughing at us or not. I offer a hand. "Come on. Let's get over to that table."

She stares at me for a long second before taking the hand. Jeffrey rushes over to pick up her abandoned beach bag and towel. I watch as she tests her ankle with a little weight before grimacing.

"Elevate the leg," I suggest. "They're always saying that in health class, right? Mrs. Honea will be back in just a second."

Jeffrey sets Avery's stuff down on the table. I try to catch his eye. His cheeks are bright red, but he doesn't make eye contact with me now. He's clearly still trying to process what I said to the cashier. I know I can't make up for it with Avery listening, so I focus on her instead. She's looking across the courtyard. I follow her gaze and see that most of her cheerleading friends are over there.

None of them come over to check on her.

And then I see why: Jordan Lyles. He's sporting his normal, larger-than-life personality. Avery looks back at me. "I'm fine," she says. "Seriously. You can go eat lunch."

I frown before realizing she's not going to talk in front of Jeffrey.

"Why don't you wait at the table?" I say to him. "I'll be over in a second."

The words slip out before I can even regret them. Jeffrey doesn't look at me. His cheeks manage to turn a slightly deeper shade of red. He marches off without a word. My heart sinks as all the pieces click together. It's more than just the embarrassing comment about not being his girlfriend. As he walks away, I realize the potion's spell has faded.

The threads of magic linking us are gone. It's almost like my dismissal sealed the effect. Jeffrey crosses the courtyard to join DeSean. He doesn't look back. I know I've got a lot of explaining to do, and the only thing I'm thankful for is that he'll be with DeSean and Sophie eating lunch for the next thirty minutes. I have time to make it right.

"I'm really fine," Avery says again. "You can go eat."

She takes a deep breath, avoiding eye contact. The last

time we talked was right after Jordan broke up with her. Right now, I know she needs a friend. There's a part of me that doesn't want to be that friend. It hurt when she left. We were best friends. For some reason, something Grammy always says echoes in my mind: *When you think about it, forgiveness is its own sort of magic.*

"Are you okay?"

Avery looks at me. I'm pretty sure she knows I'm not asking about the ankle. She glances back over at Jordan's table and shrugs. Any other time I'd let it go, walk back over to my *real* friends, but Grammy's advice shines in my mind like sunlight.

"I mean it, Avery. Are you doing okay?"

She makes an annoyed noise, but says, "I'm fine. I guess. It's frustrating. Everyone likes him more. If he's not around, it's normal. We're best friends or whatever. But when Jordan's there?"

I find myself nodding, because I know the feeling. Her friends forget about her, the same way she tried to forget about us. I force myself to take a deep breath rather than saying that out loud. Grammy is always telling me to be better than my worst thoughts.

"You know, Jordan Lyles hasn't memorized the names and distances of every habitable planet," I say quietly. That was her sixth-grade science project. "He doesn't know all the best ice cream flavors. And I'm a hundred percent certain he can't play the *Frozen* theme song on his recorder. He was lucky you even gave him the time of day, Avery."

I watch as her expression brightens. I can feel how the cobwebs in my own bitter heart are dusted off by saying something nice for once. It feels like a step in the right direction.

Avery's a little teary-eyed as she speaks. "I'm sorry. It's like—I don't know. It was easier to start over. After our fight . . ." She shakes her head. "And everything that was going on with my parents. I'm not stupid. I know it wasn't really your Grammy's fault. My parents were fighting all the time before that. It was easier to blame her . . . and to blame you."

I force myself to nod. "I think I understand. What you said to me . . ." Broke my heart? Made me question something I've been waiting for my entire life? It's hard to explain exactly how I feel without making her feel even worse, and I don't want that. "What you said hurt my feelings, but I get why you said it."

My response surprises Avery. It's like she was expecting me to walk away or call her a bad name. "I'm sorry," she repeats. "You're not a freak. The whole magic thing . . . I was thinking about you the other day. You know you told me all about it when we were little, right?"

I frown at her. "What?"

She smiles. "I'll never forget. It was when we were like five years old. I told you I wanted to be a veterinarian when I'm older. And you said you wanted to be a grandmother."

I can't help laughing. "Really?"

She nods. "It was so funny. I asked you why, and you said that on your 4,444th day you'd get your first prophetic vision. I didn't even know what *prophetic* meant! I had to look it up later. But you told me your Grammy helped people. She looked into the future and used what she learned to make their lives better. I guess . . . that's why I got so mad. When I found out my mom was going to visit her, I was hoping she'd fix everything . . ."

Now I really do understand.

"But she didn't," I say. "We can see the future. It doesn't mean we can change it."

Avery nods. "So . . . did it happen? Day 4,444? Did your powers kick in or whatever?"

I almost laugh. It's the conversation I'd always imagined we would have. Best friends talking through things—even talking through magic—like it was as normal as a blue sky.

"If you had any idea what I've been through, Avery." I shake my head. "I've spent the last month saving Jeffrey Johnson's life over and over again. . . ."

Saying his name draws my eyes back to our table. Sophie is watching us with obvious concern. DeSean looks like he's trying to keep her distracted. I know they probably don't want anything to do with Avery, but this conversation feels like a step in the right direction. I'm thinking about how good it would be to have her back when a missing detail hits me like a strike of lightning.

Jeffrey.

He's not at the table. I bolt to my feet. My stomach heaves. Avery makes a surprised noise as I sprint away, crossing the courtyard, almost slipping a few times. Sophie raises one eyebrow, like she's about to let me have it for talking to Avery, but my question cuts her off.

"Jeffrey. Where did Jeffrey go?"

I'm looking around the rest of the courtyard. Maybe he went up to get our order?

"He left." DeSean sounds annoyed. "With his soccer friends."

My eyes dart to their table. All the laughing boys we saw on our way into River City have vanished, lunch trays abandoned like ghosts. My heart is beating so loud and fast that I feel like everyone else can hear it. I can barely form the words.

"Which way?"

DeSean points to the same entrance we came in. I sprint through the gates of River City. The park is chaos. The sun is out. The crowds have grown. It's more than our middle school now. Families are sprawling. Other field trips add to the madness. Every few seconds, someone comes zipping out of the bottom of one of the tunneled slides, splashing violently into the waiting jaws of the water.

All I can think about is Jeffrey. I rejected him. I'm the reason he went running off with his soccer buddies. And now he's out here with no idea how much danger he's in.

My eyes search and search and search.

But Jeffrey is gone.

CHAPTER TWENTY-EIGHT

Teamwork

The crowd is impossible.

I'm about to just pick a direction and start running, but the more I scan my surroundings, the clearer it is that this isn't going to work. There is no way I'm going to find Jeffrey without help. I chew on my bottom lip, hesitating for a second, and sprint back into River City.

DeSean and Sophie are still at the table.

"I need your help!"

Sophie rolls her eyes. "Celia, I get that you like him, but . . ."

"It's not that. It's my magic."

I try to keep my voice low so that no one else can hear, but it still feels like the most ridiculous thing I've ever said. DeSean's eyebrow rises so high that he looks like a real-life meme. Sophie knows a little about my family, but she's still caught off guard by the word *magic*.

"Look. It's hard to explain. I've been saving Jeffrey's life. That's how I got to know him. I keep—I've been saving him. He was supposed to die over a month ago."

DeSean blinks at that.

Sophie starts to nod. "Okay. That's super weird, but at least it explains why you noticed Jeffrey in the first place. I've been trying to figure out why you two even started talking."

"That's why," I say. "And it's supposed to happen again today. At the park. I have to find him and save him."

I'm waiting for both of them to laugh in my face, but DeSean glances over at Sophie. She's still nodding. I sigh in relief when she launches into full-on action mode.

"Okay. We know he's with the soccer players." Sophie frowns. "But . . . everyone is wearing the same shirts."

"Wait," DeSean says. "I have an idea."

He scrambles to unzip a waterproof pouch. My heart is racing as he scrolls back through his pictures. This is taking too long. I'm wasting time.

"There!" DeSean turns the phone. "Everett Willis."

I stare at him. "But we're looking for Jeffrey!"

He taps the screen. "And Jeffrey is with Everett! Look at that bright red bandanna he's wearing. Most of them have one on! I didn't see anyone else wearing them. Let's start searching the park. Keep an eye out for red. Plus Everett has bright, bleached-blond hair. He should be the easiest one to spot."

All three of us start back into the park. Both of them reach the crowd I was so overwhelmed by before, but Sophie doesn't get overwhelmed.

"DeSean. Check the Wave Pool. Meet back here."

He darts off in that direction.

"Celia. We need eyes up there."

She points. There are stairs leading up to the slides. The upper platform is nearly five stories high. My feet start moving that way before I even realize it's the right decision. Of course. It's the highest vantage point in the park. I can also check if Jeffrey's in line.

"Meet back here!" Sophie shouts.

As I sprint in that direction, a sharp whistle sounds.

The lifeguard calls for me to slow down. I make a show of walking until a swirl of bodies cuts me off from sight, and I dart forward again. Groups are making their way up the stairs in threes or fours. I slip around them, hurtling up one flight after the next. At the top, a long line halts my progress. It takes less than a breath to make the decision. I push my way forward.

Complaints sound immediately.

"Just trying to find someone!" I explain. "I'm not going down the slide."

I force a path through. A few park employees are barking orders on the opposite end of the platform, sending people down the different slides. A group of boys chants another school's motto. None of the soccer players are up here. Neither is Jeffrey.

I shove back toward the platform corner that overlooks

the park. The view is dizzying. I take a deep and calming breath, refocusing on why I came up here in the first place. Jeffrey is out there somewhere. All I have to do is find him.

Except the park is like a massive, live-action version of *Where's Waldo?* It takes effort to channel Mom's approach to problem solving. Deep breath. Take on the challenge by focusing on one thing at a time. I start in the far-right corner, scanning the seating areas. It's mostly families. My eyes land on the Wave Pool next. I can see DeSean standing there at the edge, and I decide to skip it. If Jeffrey's there, he'll see him.

"Come on," I whisper to myself. "Where are you. . . ."

There's a splash zone full of little kids. Not there. Maybe he came down the slides while I was coming up? But the exit pools show no signs of the soccer players. I'm getting impatient, but I force myself to take it section by section. I squint at the line of folks by the Go-Kart track. There's not a red soccer bandanna in sight.

Panic is rising in my chest.

My eyes sweep left. From my angle, it's the one section of the Lazy River that's visible. And there's movement. A woman is pulling herself out of the water. She gestures downriver, looking annoyed. I'm too far up to hear what she's saying, but my gaze follows hers.

There.

At the far bend in the river, a fleet of inner tubes. Jeffrey isn't the first one I spot. DeSean's plan works. Everett Willis is there, his blond hair shining like a beacon. I recognize Tyreek and a few others, too. About seven boys are navigating the water, controlling way too many inner tubes. They've stacked them up like some kind of makeshift pirate ship. I can only watch as my worst fear comes to life.

They're playing a game. Boarding each other's tubes. Knocking each other into the water. It's king of the hill, but *in* the water. I can see Jeffrey at the very center of their game, splashing someone who's trying to flip his tube. And then the river sweeps them out of sight.

CHAPTER TWENTY-NINE

Death's Instrument

I sprint back down the stairs, almost decking one of our school's cheerleaders in the process. It takes effort to focus and bring up the maps I studied of the park.

The Lazy River circles around the entire water area. It's massive. I remember lifeguard stands at three different locations on the river, but I also marked a clear blind spot on the section they're heading toward. That means two things. It's where they can break the most rules, and it's where Jeffrey will be in the most danger.

Sophie and DeSean are waiting near the landing.

"Did you see him?" she calls.

"Lazy River!" I point to the right. "DeSean, why don't you go that way? Sophie, get tubes. We can jump in and try to catch up with them."

I'm surprised how quickly they both respond. DeSean sprints off, earning a whistle for his troubles. Sophie finds the nearest stack of tubes and starts searching for one that's our size. I'm watching it all, still panicking a little, when I remember there's a shortcut.

In my mind, it's a small black line that runs beneath the raised slide platforms. It connects to the back of the Lazy River. Instinct has me turning, cutting through the crowd, heading for the spot.

The sight pulls me up short. It isn't an open-entrance walkway like I thought. There's a closed door and a sign that clearly warns: EMPLOYEES ONLY!

I glance over. The lifeguard is distracted. There aren't any other employees in sight. I sneak forward and find the door unlocked. The door opens into a well-lit but narrow corridor. On either side, there are huge cages of stored inner tubes and towels. I sprint to the other end.

The door opens into too-bright sunshine. I'm on a ledge that's a foot or two above the Lazy River. Across the way, there's a quiet "beach" area where several adults have claimed chairs away from most of the chaos. A hip-high railing separates me from the water. I shove up against it and lean out as far as I can to get a better view.

Down to my left, DeSean is there. He's really far away, though, working his way up a circular walkway. My eyes cut the other way, and . . .

. . . the boys are there.

Less than one hundred yards away, floating slowly toward my position. Jeffrey is at the very top of the flotilla. He looks like the king of the hill, upper body sticking out of a stack of tubes that's three-high. Even from here, I can see him using his leverage to push away one of the other soccer players. It looks like they're just trying to have some fun.

Intuition slams into me.

I am a seer, from a family of seers. I was born knowing what comes next. I know suddenly that this is the moment

I've been waiting for. This was the vision that was taken from me. My sight doubles. The real world is still there: the park and the sky and the sunlight. But I also see another world layered over it. Black strings rope through the air, thick and knotted. Each one is attached to Jeffrey.

Death is here with us. Beckoning Jeffrey into the great beyond.

I clench my jaw and start climbing over the railing. The boys are just twenty yards downstream from my location. Jeffrey shoves another boy away from his stack of tubes. There's a massive splash. He's still laughing when he spots me on the bank.

His eyes light up in surprise.

Maybe he knows I came looking for him, even if he doesn't know why. All the embarrassment from before is gone. I'm close enough to see the freckles on the bridge of his nose. He starts to wave at me.

At that exact moment, one of the other boys shouts a clipped warning. I can see death's next move before it happens. On the opposite bank, there's a row of fake palm trees.

They double as umbrellas for the beach chairs beneath them. Each one stands about fifteen feet high, as wide as telephone poles.

My vision focuses on the one nearest the parking lot. I can see the base is cracking. Maybe it's been falling apart for years. But it chooses this exact moment to crumble because death is guiding everything with its steady hand. The base cracks. It's like a tree snapping in two. The whole column topples toward the Lazy River, and it's aimed right at Jeffrey.

Too late, I realize that I am one of death's instruments. The other soccer players all scramble to abandon their tubes, diving out of the way. Jeffrey doesn't see the threat coming because he's too busy looking at me. From up in his make-shift tower of tubes, he smiles like he'll live forever.

And the massive palm tree falls like a thunderclap.

It's not a direct blow. It doesn't crush him. But the downward swing is enough to knock him out cold. Jeffrey's upper body recoils from the impact. His lower half, however, is still stuck inside the tubes. He falls backward, his eyes closing, and all three tubes flip, following his momentum. My heart stops beating.

He's unconscious, upside down, under the water. Surrounded by the other tubes. Only his feet are visible now. The other soccer players are swimming to shore, and I can tell from their laughter that they didn't see what happened to Jeffrey as they escaped. Only I did.

There's no time to think. I dive into the water and make my second mistake. I forgot to take off my shirt before jumping. The fabric takes on water, slowing me down, as I frantically search below the surface of the water. Jeffrey is there. His entire body is flipped upside down, head almost grazing the bottom of the Lazy River.

No, no, no . . .

The river pulls us downstream. Holding my breath, I take two quick strokes. The movement brings me to Jeffrey's side. It's almost like he fell through ice on a frozen lake. All the tubes are stacked overhead. They shifted as the other boys escaped, leaving only a few places to pop back up and take a breath.

My first thought is to get Jeffrey out of the tubes. It's awkward, but I try to pull on his swimsuit and wedge him free. He doesn't even budge. The tube is way too small. It's for someone half his age, and he's jammed in impossibly tight.

Panicking, I move on to my second idea. I get a grip on his shoulders and try to flip him back upright. He shifts a little, but there are too many tubes surrounding his on the surface. Pressed together so tight that they won't move an inch.

My heartbeats are coming in triples. In my second sight, I can still see the black threads wrapped around him, coiling tighter, dark with intent. Unexpectedly, one of those threads lashes out and wraps around my wrist. I feel my limbs getting tired. My chest tightening.

And that's when the pull of the current vanishes.

It's like someone turned off the Lazy River. Can they do that? Did a lifeguard spot us? I'm still holding tight to Jeffrey as I squint upward. The light is all wrong.

Sunlight was slashing across the surface a moment before. Now there's an amber glow. That isn't the only change. The floor was a generic tan-colored cement. I blink down. Is that carpet?

I don't want to leave Jeffrey, but my body is begging me to take a breath. Just one. If I can take that breath, I'll be able to help him. I have to do it. I guide myself up through the nearest tube.

Bursting free, I gasp in a lungful of air.

The sight that greets me is impossible. I'm thinking I should shout for help, but all I can do is look around. The open sky is gone. Instead, I'm in a closed room. There are walls. A ceiling. There are lamps glowing in opposite corners. There's even a bed.

This isn't real.

My eyes settle on a familiar rocking chair and the person sitting in it. A single word bursts out of the chaos of my mind and echoes across the water. "Grammy?"

I wonder if I've died. I'm clinging to an inner tube at the very center of Grammy's room. There is no mistaking the woman who smiles at me. Her lower half is hidden by the water. In fact, the whole room is obscured from the waist down. It's like the Lazy River has teleported to our townhome for a brief, impossible moment.

What is *happening*?

Grammy rises. There's magic in the set of her shoulders, the purse of her lips. I can almost see the trace of her spells like great threads of gold weaving through the air. She walks forward and her dress trails along the surface of the water. It takes a second for my brain to remember that Jeffrey is dying. He's down under the water.

Panic has me diving again.

He's still there.

Still drowning.

Only when I try to swim forward, I can't. I push my hands out, but it's like I'm inside a massive glass fish tank. A barrier is keeping me from saving him. Anger pulses through me. It's not hard to figure out that this has something to do with Grammy's magic. I can't believe it.

She's stopping me from rescuing him.

I want to scream, but all I can do is hold my breath and watch as her slippered feet glide through the water. Grammy dives. I'm surprised how graceful her motions are, how young she looks. Memory thunders. She's been taking water aerobics classes, hasn't she?

She swims to Jeffrey. Her magic brightens when she touches his skin. One of the black threads unravels from his neck. And then a second from his arm. She takes her time. I can't help feeling like she's moving too slowly to save him.

Grammy doesn't panic. She is patient; her magic is thorough.

I don't know how much time passes, but every dark thread unwinds at her touch. Grammy is careful to collect them all, and in the end, it looks like she's holding the leashes of twenty different dogs, ready for a walk through our neighborhood. She circles Jeffrey once more, just to make sure that she has them all.

And then surfaces.

My lungs beg me to do the same. I splash through the inner tube as Grammy makes her way back to the rocking chair in the corner. She holds the black threads in her right hand. I can see them trying to sneak out of her grasp, but she doesn't allow that. Her grip is firm.

"Grammy!" I shout breathlessly. "What happened? How are you doing this?"

She doesn't answer. Instead, she lowers herself gingerly back into the rocking chair. It's the first time I've ever noticed her body's age. Her eyes tighten with pain before opening, settling on me. The look she throws my way is one of boundless pride.

"Oh, Celia," she whispers. "What a wonder you are."

Sunlight flickers. Noise from another world statics through. I can feel the tug of the Lazy River on my limbs again. And it's in that moment that I finally realize what she's done.

What she's about to do.

Grammy studies me. It's clear she sees me in the here and now, but she also sees some future version of me. That's always been her gift. Whatever she sees there has her smiling.

"You are going to live such a wondrous life. I just know it."

She lifts the black threads into the air. Her grip tightens as she presses all that darkness to her own chest. The threads start to coil around her. I get a final glimpse of her smile before the sound and the pain and the brightness of Jungle Rapids all roar back to life.

Grammy is gone.

Jeffrey's waist slips out of the tube. I drag him away, kicking double. DeSean is there to help me. Sophie is shouting for people to get out of the way up on the bank. A lifeguard is there too. He helps us out of the water and puts an ear to Jeffrey's chest. He pumps twice, and a great cough draws the water from Jeffrey's lungs. He blinks back to life.

The other soccer players rush forward, crowding around, whispering and shouting all at once. I saved Jeffrey Johnson again, but as I lean against the nearest wall for support, I realize that I'm crying. Two things could not be any clearer in this moment.

I know the first one is that Jeffrey Johnson is finally safe. For good.

The second one . . . Grammy . . .

I fight against the thought. It can't be true. I have to be wrong. I shake my head, tears streaming down my cheeks, and realize once again how much it can hurt to *know* more of the truth than other people do. No matter how hard I fight the thought, I can't deny the intuition that Grammy gifted me over all these years. Right now it's confident in one other thing.

Grammy?

Grammy is gone.

CHAPTER THIRTY

The Pain of Knowing

We sit in an upstairs room, away from all the noise, waiting.

Jeffrey is thankful to be alive. I can tell it's different this time. It was one thing for a car to run off the road in his general direction. Car accidents feel like a normal thing to us. They can happen at any time if you're not careful enough. But it's another thing to have a fake palm tree knock you unconscious and underwater on a field trip. The memory of today will stick with him for a long time.

Sophie and DeSean wait with us. I can tell they're still

trying to figure out what to believe about what just happened. It's hard to pretend today was a coincidence. I'm hoping they'll stick with me even though it is a little *weird*. The fact that they're here is a pretty good sign.

The only surprise in the room is Avery.

She slipped in after we all were escorted up. Sophie doesn't complain. It feels odd that today of all days brought our group back together. I'm so tired that it feels like my arms are bolted down to the chair. It's hard to explain to the others. I know this should be a moment of celebration. I saved Jeffrey's life. But I also know deep down in my gut that there's more to it this time.

Jeffrey's alive . . .

. . . but the dark threads coil around Grammy.

I have to shake myself. Jeffrey notices. He's kind enough not to ask whatever question comes to mind. We're all sitting in silence when the door opens. My stomach knots up even more as Tatyana walks into the room. She comes in looking annoyed, but after glancing around the room, she raises one eyebrow. DeSean looks just as surprised as the rest of us.

"Why aren't you in school?"

"I don't have a fourth period," she throws back. "I've been waiting outside?"

He frowns at that. "But I'm going back home on the bus today."

"Not for you," Tatyana corrects. She looks at me. "Didn't you book me?"

More tangled knots in my stomach.

"No, I didn't."

Tatyana lifts one eyebrow, sliding her phone out of a back pocket. She's as fast with it as she is behind the wheel. She turns the screen and shows me our text thread. Sure enough, there's a message there from my number. Even though I know I never sent her a text.

It reads: Pick up at Jungle Rapids at 2:13. Cool?

"Super specific," Tatyana says. "Which was weird, but here I am. It's 2:13."

I don't pull my own phone out to confirm, because I can already see all the dominoes set out in their obvious pattern, all pointing to this moment. The only problem is if I touch the first one, the entire thing will fall, and I'll know the truth. A truth I don't want to accept. . . .

And then my phone rings. It's Mom.

"Celia? It's me. I'm at the hospital. . . ."

Her words rumble like thunder. It's hard to hear what she says after the word *hospital* because that word splits my heart right down the middle. I was right. Grammy . . .

". . . I can't leave her to come get you. Your aunt is too far away. I tried calling Cindy at work, but she's not picking up. So I just need you to go home after school. I'll get a hold of—"

That's why Tatyana is here. It hits me even harder. Even with her life on the line, Grammy still arranged everything so neatly. The text from my phone was sent by her. My voice whispers out.

"It's okay, Mom. Tatyana is here. DeSean's sister. She can bring us."

Mom sounds a little nervous, reminds me not to rush, but I can tell from the edge in her voice that Grammy's . . .

. . . No. I can't accept that. It can't be true.

"We're on the way."

Tatyana doesn't look confused now. She knows there's something odd about me, and rolls with it quickly enough. I'm grateful I don't have to explain. We step outside the room and find Mrs. Honea posted there like an armed guard.

"Feeling better, Celia?"

I have no answer for that. I feel like a universe is about to vanish from existence.

"Tatyana has to take me to the hospital." I can't fight the shaking in my voice. "My Grammy is there. She's in the emergency room. My mom just called."

Mrs. Honea says something about permission slips, approved drivers, all of that. Surprisingly, it's Avery who steps in and explains. She talks Mrs. Honea through it all, pointing out that I definitely should go. Jeffrey's not under my spell anymore, but he stays glued to my side as we descend the stairs. All the back and forth happens in whispers. I don't listen because the truth is waiting ahead, in the dark distance.

A hospital room. My favorite person in the world.

"I can't let the rest of you go," Mrs. Honea is saying.

"Celia has permission directly from her mother. The rest of you have to stay here. I can't just send students to a hospital unattended."

Jeffrey fights back. "You could drive us. Or come with us? That way we have a chaperone."

Sophie jumps in too. I'm so thankful for them, but right now all I can feel is the slow-motion collapse of my entire world. The front doors of the building open, and I stumble out into the carpool lane, sunlight shining on my skin like a bright lie.

"Celia, this way."

Tatyana wraps an arm around my shoulder, guiding me to her car. There's distant arguing still. I can hear Mrs. Honea correcting someone. Tatyana helps me into the back seat, puts a belt around me, and gets the engine revving.

There's a little commotion back by the entrance as Tatyana shifts gears and swings the car around. I catch Mrs. Honea with her back to us, trying to explain something to Sophie, who's clearly making a scene now. As she does, Jeffrey backpedals quietly. When he's out of our teacher's line of sight, he turns and signals to Tatyana. She slows enough for him to get around the other side of the car and slide into the back seat. Mrs. Honea turns too late, hearing the car door close, as we speed off with him inside. No one speaks.

Tatyana guides our car to the only hospital on this side of town. Everything outside rushes past in dizzying blurs. Jeffrey reaches across the seat. I bury my hand in his. It helps the spinning, nauseous feeling. Ambulances are parked outside. Tatyana navigates the light traffic before swinging right in front of the emergency room doors.

"I'll wait in the parking lot," she says. Then to Jeffrey, "You got her?"

He nods back. My arms and legs still don't seem to be working. He comes around to help me out, linking an arm with mine.

"We need to get you some food," he says. "After we find the right room."

It's what you'd expect from a hospital.

A bunch of folks sprawled inside too-bright waiting

rooms. Jeffrey leads us to the nearest help desk, and my vision spins a little. I'm *feeling* too much. I can tell because my second sight is surging in quick-burst visions. I can smell campfires everywhere. The glimpses don't cut me away from the world the way Jeffrey's always do. Instead, I see people transform before my very eyes. A little girl playing with blocks stands up, fully grown, dressed in a business suit and wearing dark-framed glasses.

A pregnant mother with one hand set on her stomach shifts in her seat, and two little girls appear—one on either side of her—smiling at the woman whose face mirrors the same love for them. Little futures sprout from every chair, some darker than others, but all spinning like magic. Jeffrey barely keeps me standing.

"Let's get some water," he says. "She's right down the hall. Room 4120."

He fills up a cup. I avoid looking at all the people in the waiting room, because seeing their futures is draining me faster than running a marathon. Jeffrey lets me take a few sips before guiding me down toward the wing where

Grammy should be. One right, a long walk, and then a left. Room 4120. I take a deep breath before entering. Mom is there. Grammy's clothes are neatly folded in a corner chair. Her bed is empty.

"Mom?"

She looks up from her phone, face streaked with tears. "Oh, Celia. They just took her into surgery. I—I don't understand all of it. She's not doing well. A lot of internal issues. The doctor . . ."

Her arms open and I disappear into a hug. There's no way to hold her tight enough, no way to push back against the truth. Mom won't understand. She doesn't know I've been saving Jeffrey, or that Grammy knew all about it. I sink into the chair with her, which squeezes us tight together, and I let my head rest on her shoulder.

Jeffrey introduces himself before moving to the opposite corner. He doesn't mention the fact that I saved his life today, but it's all I can think about now. Tatyana's arrival was like another piece to a puzzle I didn't know I was supposed to solve. The pieces link together now, and the image that forms has me more afraid for Grammy than ever. I know she's in the doctor's hands now. There's nothing I can do to save her, but like anyone would, I replay all the moments that led to now.

The first truth is that she *knew*.

She clearly planned everything that happened, which means she knew how and when Jeffrey would die. That drags me back to when I had the incomplete vision. I got that glimpse of Jeffrey and it felt like I'd been knocked backward, away from my second sight.

What happened next?

I can't believe I didn't see it. I walked into the house, completely panicking, and Grammy was kneeling on the floor. She pretended to be checking the cookies in the oven. The realization is stunning. I never lost the vision. My second sight didn't just slip out of my hands.

Grammy took it from me. On purpose.

So Grammy saw how Jeffrey would die. The Cleary Family Guide Book said that visions could be traded to someone else. I guess I always thought it would require my permission. Grammy obviously knew something I didn't. That makes sense. She's been doing this prophecy thing for sixty years. It wouldn't be hard for her to outmuscle me and steal my vision.

Or my binding spell, for that matter.

That's realization number two. I *know* I made enough tea. I am my mother's daughter. Every detail just so. There was plenty of the mixture for two cups. The idea that anything—magical or not—could boil down that much? There's no chance that happened.

Grammy must have taken some for herself after I went to bed. I'm mostly guessing, but I imagine it would create a link between all three of us. I have no idea how she was powerful enough to draw the Lazy River back to her room in the townhome, but it's pretty clear that the link she used was the one I created.

After that, she sent the text to Tatyana.

I pull out my phone and glance at the timestamp. Sent at 4:44 a.m. I bury my face in my hands. I can envision her slipping into my room, walking over to the nightstand where my phone always charges. She texted Tatyana because she *knew* what she was doing wouldn't end well. She knew Mom wouldn't be able to come get me *and* stay with her. She was prepared for all of it.

But the last truth is the hardest one.

Grammy found a way to save Jeffrey. There's only one way she could have figured it out. The missing page. The one she tore out decades ago. She told me she hadn't read it, and knowing Grammy, she was likely telling the truth. At least, in that moment she was.

I'd bet anything that she went and read the page as soon as we finished our walk. I'm certain it had the answer she was hoping to find. The answer she used to save him.

I can even imagine the words written in the book.

It's possible for a life to be sacrificed in exchange for another.

It feels right, because that's so clearly what Grammy did. I watched her take each of those deathly threads attached to Jeffrey. She was so thorough about it. And so purposeful when she placed them on herself instead.

Oh, Celia. What a wonder you are.

Mom holds me tighter as I start to cry.

About thirty minutes later, a doctor enters the room.

"Ms. Cleary? Could we speak in private?"

Those words translate in midair, spinning out like little shadows. I hear the words his question tries to hide, words that we're not taught to speak, that no one can help us to accept.

Your life? It will never, ever be the same.

CHAPTER THIRTY-ONE

A Most Bizarre Funeral

I develop a quick and thorough hatred of the past tense.

Every time Mom says the words *Grammy was* instead of *Grammy is*. The way visitors smile and say—as if we are co-conspirators—*well, you know how she was*. All the bridge players who've fluttered up our front steps to tell us exactly what they *loved* about Grammy. The past tense is nothing more than a slight alteration. Each time it's a whispered reminder that Grammy is gone.

In the nights after she passes, I don't sleep well.

Friends visit during the day. Their presence keeps the

sadness smaller, but at night I'm alone enough to start feeling guilty. Guilty because in a way, I'm the one who caused Grammy's death. It was my vision that dragged her into this. It was my stubborn decision to keep saving Jeffrey. Now that she's really gone, I slowly convince myself that it was all *my* fault.

It's only natural that Grammy's still the one whispering advice to me from the grave. On the second night, I crept downstairs and into her room. I pulled down the covers and crawled into the spot where I used to sleep when I was a little girl, tucked against her generous frame.

As a new wave of guilt crashed over me, Grammy's voice thundered out in answer. It was so sharp and present that I sat up and looked around for her. She wasn't there, but a memory of her was. When I was a little girl, she'd pulled me aside at the park to teach me about forgiveness after a particularly annoying boy broke one of my toys.

Her favorite quote on the subject went like this: *Forgiveness is the fragrance the violet sheds on the heel that crushed it.* Back then, I didn't like the idea of anyone *crushing* a flower. It seemed like such a rude thing to do. Now the meaning of what she said washed back over me.

I am the heel.

Grammy is the violet.

It shouldn't surprise me that her fragrance is everywhere. This room is a small universe she shaped to her liking. Every pillow, every color, every indentation, is a reminder. I fall asleep with the strange assurance that she forgives me.

A whispered voice reminds me there is nothing to forgive.

We get ready for the funeral. I'm wearing a black dress that Grammy bought me last summer. I remember trying it on. She thought the flowing sleeves made me look on the verge of flight. Some small part of me wonders if she picked it out with the funeral in mind. It's harder than ever to tell what she saw and didn't see of the future that was coming.

Either way, the dress is an easy choice. Mom's having a harder time.

I can hear her switching into her third dress choice,

muttering under her breath the whole time. Something about Grammy abandoning her to speak in front of a bunch of random relatives. I can't help imagining Grammy across the living room, sitting in her chair, winking at me.

It is the first funeral I've ever attended. It starts exactly the same way I've been taught in movies. A large room with pews. Everyone in dark clothes. Hushed voices and sideways glances. Grammy lies in an elegant coffin with her hands folded.

I feel a touch dizzy seeing her that way, but when I look closer, it almost looks like there's a smirk on her face. I'm not sure if it's my imagination or some trick of the light, but something about her planning one final joke for us all feels comforting.

Other family members file into the room behind us. Mary and Martha take seats to my right. Mary throws a comforting arm around my shoulder as Aunt Corabel plunks in beside them.

More family members fill up the rows. Looking back, I

spy Jeffrey, Sophie, DeSean, and Avery walking down the main aisle together. Jeffrey offers his quiet smile.

Only when every row is filled, and the stragglers have settled, does the funeral director step out onto the raised stage beyond Grammy. He stands behind an old-fashioned podium.

I'm surprised by how uncomfortable he looks. It's odd. You'd kind of think that he'd be used to this sort of thing by now. After all, his job title is *funeral director*.

He clears his throat. "Uhh, okay, welcome. We are here to celebrate the life of Estelle Cleary. I've—well, I've been instructed to begin with a letter from the deceased. It was delivered to me several weeks ago with express instructions to be read aloud. In front of all of you."

The crowd grows quiet.

Not everyone knows the extent of Grammy's talents. I'd guess many of her friends thought that visions were something she dabbled in, almost like a fun and amusing pastime. I can see curious looks up and down the rows. Our family, however, knows this is going to get really weird really fast.

The director glances briefly at Grammy's coffin, almost as if he's watching for signs of movement. After an awkward pause, he continues.

"And now a word from Estelle Cleary. 'Good morning! I do hope that I look as lovely as all of you do. What an honor to have you. I wanted to begin by thanking each and every person who came here to honor my memory. Yes, that even means you, Larry Connors. Never could get to bingo on time, could you?'"

An uncomfortable silence follows.

The back doors of the room close with a thump. Our attention is drawn that way. An older man stands there, frozen in an attempt to finish tucking in his shirt, his eyes wide as moons. Nervous laughter sounds. A lot of people look confused. The man—Larry Connors, apparently—waves an apology as if Grammy's standing at the front of the room scolding him.

"'I do think the flowers look lovely,'" the director continues. "'A hat tip to the Garland sisters. I liked the hydrangeas so much that I decided to steal some for myself.'"

That has every neck craning. I hadn't noticed at first glance, but she does have a single clutch of blue flowers set gracefully beneath her lifeless hands. The beginning of a grin tugs at my face as the director keeps reading. Beads of sweat run down his forehead.

"'I've got a hundred bucks on Ellen Johnson crying first. Don't you worry, Ellen. I've got a good feeling you'll find someone to sip tea with you on Tuesdays.'"

There's a little outburst of tears on the opposite side of the aisle. An older woman I recognize shakes her head, half laughing at the accuracy of Grammy's words.

"'I was surprised the cousins from Tallahassee came up. You're too sweet, the lot of you. Make sure not to take I-95 home, though. Oh! And little Elena, I do adore that red dress . . . As for you, Evelyn, didn't I tell you . . .'"

It doesn't take long for the entire room to start laughing. It's not a competition, but I feel like I'm laughing louder than anyone. The letter is one hand-picked prophecy after the next. I can only imagine how much time she spent preparing all this. Maybe she touched objects in each of their houses or cars over the decades, carefully gathering this information for one final joke. There are comments on haircuts and untied shoes, and even one line about a bridge club member who'd forgotten his dental appointment. Grammy instructed him to leave now or else he'd have to fork up fifty dollars for a missed-appointment fee.

I'm smiling so hard that my face starts to hurt. Grammy's final act is a reminder to me. I can feel the words whispering in the air above us. I am a seer, born into a family of seers.

Embrace this, Grammy seems to be saying. *Walk into this world of magic and explore every inch of it. Do not hide from these gifts, my dear. Never pretend to be less than you are. You are my granddaughter. That means the future is in your hands. Make something wonderful out of it.*

The director uses a handkerchief to wipe sweat from his forehead. The entire room is still laughing at the list of impossible predictions. As the director reaches the end, my uncle Clay actually gets to his feet a few rows back and roars out to the director.

"Can someone give her shoulders a shake? I mean, are we even sure . . ."

Now the director's face blushes to a plumlike color.

"I want to make sure it's clear that these are Estelle's words, sir," he says. "Not mine. But she states rather clearly in the letter that I should, 'Tell Clay to sit back down. He can talk to me when he wears a suit that's from this century.'"

Clay's burst of laughter leads the rest of the room. He nearly collapses back onto one of my little cousins, his face red with the delight at Grammy's final dig. The director eventually has to hold up one hand to settle the group back down.

"Well, the rest of the letter is a bit more . . . sincere. This part is for the Cleary family." He folds the upper half back to begin reading. "'You all knew—better than most— that this day would come. Even in our rather talented family, death remains undefeated. I accepted that reality long ago and began picking my battles accordingly. I could not defeat death, but I made sure to win as often as possible in the game of life.

"'Look around. I think I did all right. There are close friends in this crowd. People who celebrated *and* mourned with me. There are bright smiles of grandchildren. An entire world that we created together. I would rather not think of this as an ending, but as the beginning of something new. It is your chance—each and every one of you—to take the world I began and make it into whatever you'd like it to be. I find that thought calming. For I have seen how steady the hands are into which I am placing my one precious world. Do your best to make it more magical. I trust all of you will find yourselves capable of that.'"

A solemn quiet follows.

The director folds the letter, and that is about how long it takes for my smile to fade. It was a really funny joke. I'm sure Grammy was planning it for a while now, but as I watch them close her coffin and my uncles walk forward to help carry it out, I realize this was Grammy's *last* joke. It's a hard thought to swallow. We all turn and watch as her coffin is ferried down the main aisle.

All her magic seems to go with her.

CHAPTER THIRTY-TWO

Only Just Beginning

After the burial, we return home. Mary and Martha claim the guest room. Aunt Corabel crashes with Mom, and both of them pass out almost immediately. I'm sitting in the quiet of the empty kitchen when my eyes land on the Cleary Family Guide Book.

It isn't on the chair where I left it.

Instead, the book sits on the table directly across from me. Light from the windows slashes across the cover like a spotlight. I stare at it for a long time. I can't help wondering if Grammy left it there on purpose. All the details have lined up so far. The water aerobics classes she'd been taking. Her text to Tatyana. It feels like I'm trying to catch up to someone who lived her life twelve steps ahead of everyone else.

I reach across the table, pulling the book to me, and open it.

A loose page flutters out. I don't need to look at it to know that this is the missing page Grammy kept from me. Taking a breath, I unfold it. My eyes trace the text, landing on words like *sacrifice* and *shifting death's attention*. It confirms what I guessed. I find a sticky note attached down at the bottom of the page. Grammy's handwriting stares up at me:

You've probably figured it out by now, Celia.
You've always been clever. Well, I finally
figured it out too. The vision I had all those
decades ago was about you and Jeffrey. We
all thought that ripping out the page would
be enough to save you, but some futures are

stubborn like that. Deep roots that require a sturdy shovel. I do not want you to blame yourself. Jeffrey was always destined to die. I never guessed that you'd be willing to sacrifice your own life for his. But I saw a confirmation of my worst fears when I stole your vision. You were going to save him, Celia. One final time. And the cost would have been your own life. Death found that trade acceptable and had every intention of claiming my most beloved granddaughter.

Naturally, I could not allow that.

You were always going to save him, and I was always going to save you.

Some futures are clearer than others. This particular moment was set into motion decades ago. Please do not ever feel guilty for having a good heart. We only have the choices we make, and one of the best choices I've ever made was you.

You saved him, Celia. We saved him.

I could not think of a better way to retire.

And there's the truth of it, plain as day. Grammy sensed—all those years ago—that if I were ever allowed to read this page, I'd sacrifice myself for Jeffrey. I'm not sure if she's right. It isn't an easy thing to die. Maybe I would have saved him without thinking about it, though. Set my life down for his, simply because I couldn't stand by and watch him die. I start to cry again when I realize Grammy made that choice so I wouldn't have to.

More tears trickle down as I notice handwriting *beneath* the sticky note. Grammy's sharp cursive is on the page as well. Like all the seers before her, she's made an addition. Next to the descriptions of sacrificial magic, she notes simply: *The original writer asks an important question: Who is worthy of being saved? It is no small thing for a seer to sacrifice their life, after all. But the answer is as simple as the question. The people we choose to save are made worthy by our efforts to save them. I have seen it with my own eyes.*

It takes effort to keep my breathing steady. I trace her words with a finger, as if a touch might bring her back to me. Overwhelmed, I start to close the book. But I catch another glimpse on the next page. More handwriting. Frowning, I flip through the next chapter. And the next one. And the next.

Grammy's thoughts are everywhere. She's written some directly into the guide. Pieces of advice for anyone to read: *I've found that stripping the leaves first produces clearer visions.* But there are also some sticky notes written directly to me: *Celia, I was worried you might be destined to live your life as a Grimdark or a Deathwell, but all the evidence so far points to two other categories. It is not uncommon that our more powerful family members can dabble in multiple branches, after all. I've already mentioned that you have a lot in common with Precognition Engineers. You'll find more details about that branch on page seven, but you'll want to cross-check what you find with page seventy-four as you have more visions. There's information there on Proximity Clairvoyants. The more I think about your first vision, the more I'm convinced . . .*

There are notes about ingredients. On one page she suggests wearing gloves for a certain spell. I read through everything patiently, drinking in lessons I'd thought were lost. These additions must have taken every spare hour of her time. I looked at this book the night before the field trip. How could she possibly have written all this? It must have taken her all night.

Footsteps sound in the living room.

"Oh, Celia. Don't cry, honey."

I look up as Mom crosses the room. She sees the guide book in my lap. There's a flash of concern on her face. In part because the book is a world she's never known, but she must realize too that the person meant to guide me through this other world is gone.

Carefully I wipe away the tears. She's not gone. Not really.

"She left notes for me," I whisper. "All the things she wanted to teach me."

I'm not sure Mom fully understands, but she wraps me in a hug all the same. It's breathtaking. The way Grammy thought of everything even as she saved Jeffrey. Saved me.

I sit comfortably with Mom's arm around me and turn to the very last page. There's a little scrawl of a note, and I can almost see Grammy's sly smile.

My best magic is only just beginning.

CHAPTER THIRTY-THREE

Her Final Spell

The summer heat forces our group down into the shade of the greenway. We walk without a plan, adventuring for no reason at all. Clumps of honeysuckle hang down on our right. I reach out and run a hand along the trunk of Grammy's favorite tree as we pass.

Our group feels whole now.

Sophie walks up front like a tour guide. DeSean and Jeffrey are a few steps behind her, their shoulders pressed together as they watch a video from their favorite YouTuber. I walk at the back of the group with Avery. It's so strange to have some of my life go back to normal, even though other parts of my life will never be the same without Grammy. She'd call that the *beautiful balance of life*.

Avery bumps my shoulder. "Hey. I've got some news."

I raise a curious eyebrow.

"My dad is moving back in," she says, almost embarrassed by it. "Mom said they just needed some space. Time to work it all out. It gave them both perspective."

An image comes to mind. I can see Avery's mom sitting down in the living room with Grammy. I know that Grammy would have asked for a special item. A wedding ring or a favorite book. I can picture her turning that item over in her hands, using it to glimpse the possible futures. I'd bet anything she smiled when the meeting was over and promised Avery's mom it would all be all right in the end.

"That's great, Avery."

She nods, still blushing. "And it means your Grammy was right. I thought . . . well, it doesn't matter now, I guess. Her magic helped them. Pretty cool."

We haven't talked a lot about my magic. Avery checks

in every now and again to see how it's going. Mom asks me about it sometimes, and Mary started calling me regularly. I was worried I'd end up seeing another death, but Grammy's prediction came true. My magic isn't based on one particular branch like most people. It works on proximity. I've had a few more visions now, and they're almost always of someone nearby. Someone who needs a little nudge to help them.

The only one in our crew that doesn't fully know about my magic is Jeffrey. Not yet. Sophie and DeSean agreed that it would be best if he doesn't know he was supposed to die. I don't think knowing Grammy sacrificed herself to save him would be the best introduction to the other world that's so important to me.

Our crew turns a corner on the greenway. The pond appears up on the right. Sophie heads that way, shouting something about finding a pet turtle. The group follows. Jeffrey and DeSean skip stones over the surface. Sophie recruits Avery to help build a makeshift fishing rod. I settle into a shady spot near the path. I'm sitting there, smiling at all of them, when Jeffrey sneaks back to sit with me.

"This is fun," he announces. "I never used to come down here."

Long practices in the sun have darkened his olive skin. The edges of his brown hair have spun their way to gold. I can't help eyeing him and wondering what kind of future Grammy saw that made her want to save him. Her reasoning in the journal was simpler: *You were always going to save him, and I was always going to save you.* I realize this was Grammy's final piece of magic. A group of friends hanging out at a pond. A boy with an easy smile. Her final piece of magic is happening this very moment, and it will keep happening every time Jeffrey wakes up in the morning.

"I used to walk down here with my Grammy."

He glances at me. It's quiet for a second. Sunlight dances over the water.

"Do you miss her?"

"Every day."

He nods at that. "I'm sorry, Celia. I know it's not easy. You know . . . it's the weirdest thing. It's random, but I have this memory of meeting her? Like I have a memory of talking to her and everything. I'm pretty sure I dreamed it, though."

I have to hold back a laugh. He *did* meet her. I'm sure that magical encounter feels like a dream in some distant corner of his mind. We accidentally summoned him to the house. For some reason, that feels like an appropriate way to meet someone as magical as Grammy.

A grin steals over my face.

"Let me guess. You came over to the house in the dream. We probably sat down together on the couch and watched *The Dread Files* or something like that?"

His eyes go wide. "How . . ."

"And you told me that you *really* liked me, right?"

Jeffrey's jaw is hanging open. "Uhh . . . I'm not sure I ever said . . . anything . . ."

I squint at him suspiciously before grinning.

"You're right. Probably just a dream. But if you really want to, we could go to a movie together this week." I lean in a little closer and tap my nose. "You can even tell me how much you like the freckles on my nose."

The look on his face is priceless. I stand up, brushing

grass off my shorts, and walk over to join the others. Avery and Sophie are trying to tie an old apple to the end of their fishing line. DeSean laughs as he films their efforts. Jeffrey joins the fun without hesitation, trying to play it cool, but every few seconds he grins back at me. I stand there at the edge of the water and catch a brief *glimpse*.

Movement reflects and echoes until there's another group standing on the opposite bank. I'm not sure if this is magic or not, but the five of us stand there. Everyone looks a little older, but the more I squint, the less clear the details become. I smile at that unwritten future, thankful at least that we'll get to face it together. I give a little wave, and future me waves back before vanishing. Now there's just sunlight tracing patterns on the water.

And five friends making the most of a summer day.

Most people expect seers to wear funny hats. Maybe some dark eye shadow or nails that are so long we can snatch the future out of thin air. We're expected to ride on fancy brooms or carry cast-iron cauldrons everywhere we go. Our house pets are surely spiders, and naturally, our favorite color is always black.

Sometimes, though, a seer is just the girl next door. She's starting eighth grade soon, and she's doing her best to make the world a better place, one vision at a time.

Acknowledgments

The first person I always need to thank is my wife, Katie. You are my person. If someone predicted that I'd spend the rest of my life waking up, walking downstairs, and making coffee for you, I'd tell them that they were a talented seer, and then I would pay them any sum of money they desired to make sure my life went on like that, forever. Thank you for being the greatest joy in my life.

This is the very first book I've written as the father of *three* children, instead of two. When you're old enough to read, I want to make it abundantly clear that you're all very distracting creatures who seem to have more in common with wolves than humans, but alas, I am very fond of each of you. As my momma would say, I guess I'll keep you. A special welcome to Little Scottie. The family rules are that you change your own diapers, you can't date until you're thirty, and you can't hog the Lucky Charms all for yourself. Welcome to the family.

Not many people understand the ins and outs of the publishing world. This book is my first with a new publisher. It is something of a brand-new start for me. A lot like the first day of school might feel. I could not have asked for a more gracious welcome to this next stage of my career than I had from my new editor—Anna Parsons. Thank you for believing in this story. Thank you for picking it up, combing through it, and making sure that every facet was properly shining. On our first call, I said that I loved to be edited—and I truly do. We can only take our work so far alone. I am quite glad that I had you to coax out the best possible version of this story.

We didn't achieve that alone. I'm grateful to the vision of our publisher, Valerie Garfield. A huge thanks to Sara Berko,

Jen Strada, Chloe Kuka, and Olivia Ritchie, as well as the design of Laura DiSiena. Truly, I am indebted to the entire team at Aladdin and Simon & Schuster. It is a unique sort of magic to take an idea from someone's mind and transform it into a book that other people can hold and read. I'm so grateful for the role you all played in making my dream come to life.

I also owe a book-shaped thank-you to Julie McLaughlin for bringing the cover to life. I've known Celia Cleary for years now, but something magical happens when art crosses paths with imagination. Thank you for bringing this wonderful character to life for me and all my readers.

There wouldn't have been a book to illustrate a cover for, however, without my agent, Kristin Nelson. We've been through a ton of submissions and stories together, and I'm always appreciative of your unwavering faith in me as a creator. It means the world to me, especially in the hardest moments of the writing life. Thank you to everyone at the Nelson Literary Agency for working around the clock to make the literary world a better place.

Last but not least, I will *always* thank the educators who

work so closely with me. I'm spending the first months of this book's life visiting you and your students. It is our collective privilege to transform hesitant readers into lifelong readers. I will always write my books for you and for your students. So much of what you do goes unsung, but not today. Thank you for teaming up with me. I predict—like any proper seer would—that we'll have some excited new readers on our hands when the dust settles. Let's keep inviting them to the next adventure and the next, together.

About the Author

SCOTT REINTGEN is a former public school teacher from North Carolina. He survives mostly on cookie dough, which he is told is the most important food group. When he's not writing, he uses his imagination to entertain his wife, Katie, and their three children. Scott is the author of the Nyxia Triad and the Talespinners series. You can follow him on Facebook and Instagram, and find him on Twitter @Scott_Thought.